PATRIOT DREAMS

PATRIOT DREAMS

Through Ten Generations

DAVID J. GLUNT

RESOURCE *Publications* • Eugene, Oregon

PATRIOT DREAMS
Through Ten Generations

Resource Publications
An Imprint of Wipf and Stock Publishers
199 W. 8th Ave., Suite 3
Eugene, OR 97401

www.wipfandstock.com

PAPERBACK ISBN: 978-1-5326-7586-7
HARDCOVER ISBN: 978-1-5326-7587-4
EBOOK ISBN: 978-1-5326-7588-1

Manufactured in the U.S.A.   01/31/19

Contents

Acknowledgements

THIS IS A WORK of fiction. While the characters are fictional, they are based on genealogical records beginning with Johan Jacob Klund, who immigrated to the United States in 1738. The historical incidents have been carefully researched, and quotations from historical sources are accurate throughout. The novel can be considered a reliable resource for students of American history.

I owe a huge debt of gratitude to a very distant cousin, Richard Glunt, who has researched the Klund family genealogy for some thirty years. We, together with you, owe an enormous debt to the patriots who sacrificed so much to build a future for the generations that would follow.

I must acknowledge and thank my sister Lavonne for her keen eyes and sound advice as the manuscript unfolded. Thanks also to Jordan and Jacob Wilder, two young neighbors, and to my good friend Jim Wootton who agreed to comment on the opening chapters. Finally, I also want to say a heartfelt thank you to my wife, Lois, for her support and insights throughout the process as she patiently waited for it to come to a close.

Escape

June 7, 1738—Bayern, Western Germany

"Hurry, over here in the shadows. I hear horses behind us. Yes, I have Andrew. Is your father with you? Stay low now, and be quiet until they pass."

We had left our home in the dark of night—my wife, Barbara, and my son, Andrew, along with her father and brothers. My parents, some of our other family members, and many of our friends would remain in Zweibruchen—a few because of age and illness, others who preferred a slow starvation to the perils of flight.

The last winter in the German Palatinate had been especially harsh. When the bitter cold set in, our town was already nearly without food or fuel. We also knew that the French army could march in at any time and take away our meager supplies. Like many others, we had to make a critical decision. The hope of a new life in America was accompanied by fears of the great perils along the way. Even if we were able to escape to Rotterdam, we had no assurance of passage to England or America.

Barbara held tightly to my arm as we emerged from the shadows into the street. She held onto little Andrew with her other hand. Her father and her two brothers trailed cautiously behind us. I was most concerned about Mr. Holl's ability to survive the long and difficult journey. I was also concerned about my ability to lead this escape.

In a few minutes we found a familiar path down to the river. There, waiting for us, was a small boat that Mr. Holl had purchased from a family estate just a few weeks after his wife died. I stepped in first and offered a hand to Barbara and the children. Mr. Holl climbed in last and untied the rope. I took an oar and pushed off. The stream was neither wide nor deep, but we began to glide smoothly away.

In preparation for this journey, we had sold much of our personal belongings. We now owned only what we could carry. Barbara's father questioned that. "Johan," he said, "What if we have to turn back? We will have almost nothing to begin again."

I told him that even after selling so much, we were not certain that we would have enough money to pay for all we needed, including the fare for the voyage across the Atlantic. We had done some planning. Mr. Holl had sent a letter to his friends, the Schmidt family in Pennsylvania, seeking advice and whatever help they could provide. We had no answer yet.

In a few hours it would be daylight. We prayed that no authorities would stop and question us. I had a carefully drawn map of the way to Rotterdam. It would probably take us several days to get there. The rivers would take us most of the way, but we could be stopped and questioned at any time. So, we planned to move mostly at night until we crossed the border into the Netherlands.

At daybreak, we calculated that we were nearing the city of Maastrict. We pulled the boat over under some trees along the bank and ate some bread and cheese. Barbara had brought a knapsack with enough food for two or three days. We believed we could purchase more in Rotterdam. The day passed slowly. We had time for prayer, reflection, and dreaming of a new life, but we were anxious to get back on the water. Before sunset we stepped back into the boat. Soon we would be on the Rhine with many other ships and boats. With all that traffic, we could travel in daylight with little fear of being stopped.

The next evening, flowing with the Rhine, we moved faster without incident. After a prayer of thanksgiving, we slept a few hours in a field later that night. Rotterdam was within reach the following day. We rose early and moved swiftly on the river all day, but we were not prepared for the crowded area around the city.

When we joined in the waiting crowd, we learned that the authorities would not allow us to enter Rotterdam. They feared the spread of disease from the poor and weary migrants who were gathering in the fields by the hundreds every day. After a few weary days of waiting, Dutch officials escorted us to a ship that would take us to Dover, England. We paid most of our money just for that privilege. Would we be able to afford the next fare across the Atlantic? What would happen if we could not? Only God could answer that. I closed my eyes and prayed for all of us.

CHAPTER 1

Grandma's Trunk

"Jacob!" My father sounded a little peeved that I hadn't arrived at the dinner table with everyone else. My name was still
echoing off the walls as I scampered down the stairs, trying to
compose a good excuse for being late and hoping no one asked
where I had been. "You can say grace tonight," my mom suggested, looking at me with two smiling eyes. She probably remembered the days when her own brother was twelve years old
and prone to mischief. Uncle Bill was now old enough to be my
dad, but he still had a lot of fun in him. I think Mom's family took
life less seriously than Dad's.

I said a quick and simple, "Thanks for the good food and
the hands that prepared it." That fulfilled my duty, but it probably
didn't impress anyone at the table. Least of all my sister, Liz. She
gave me a little smirk, which I tried to ignore. She could be nice at
times, so I tolerated some of her counterfeit grins and put downs.

After dinner, the four of us remained at the table for the cus-
tomary "family sharing time." Sometimes I wanted it to be over
fast, but mostly I enjoyed hearing what everybody's day was like.
Dad usually wrapped it up with a short verse or parable from the
Bible. We were what some of the neighbor kids called "religious."
Most of our neighbors went to church, at least sometimes, but we
hardly ever missed a Sunday.

I rose and set off for the attic as soon as the sharing was declared over. It was an adventure that seemed to hold great promise. I had found the back stairs to the attic soon after we moved into Grandma's house, just a few months after she passed away. I had always loved to come to this house when Grandma lived here. She was, without rival, the best cook in Pennsylvania, and she didn't think sweets were harmful to kids. Sometimes my folks let me spend a week of my summer vacation with Grandma. I got to know the "'neighborhood" kids very well, although they were scattered over a mile or two. And I usually gained a pound or more, despite the hiking, playing, and daily running around.

At first, Mom and Dad were not so certain that they wanted to keep Grandma Klund's house that they had inherited. They debated about it for a long time before making the decision not to sell it. For one thing, they didn't really want to move farther away from where Dad taught school. For another thing, they weren't sure how Liz and I would adjust to a house that reminded us of Grandma's absence every day. It hadn't been so long since we shared a lot of tears at Grandma's funeral.

Another problem was that the house needed a ton of work. We weren't rich enough to hire it done, so Dad would have to spend an evening or two each week and part of most Saturdays replacing old wood, painting, and repairing broken things. Despite all these misgivings, the house seemed to be a part of our family heritage. So, they kept it.

Liz and I weren't too keen on changing schools and making new friends if we moved. But when we did, it worked out great. The kids that lived out here in the country were friendlier than those in town. Our neighbors were farther away, but our new friends often rode their bikes to our house, and their parents were happy that we were improving the old house that Dad called Victorian.

So, I sneaked back up to the attic. I had discovered the stairs to the attic behind a door in a small room above the kitchen. We weren't using that room yet, because it needed major repairs and cleaning. Dad had told Mom "I'll get to it, but not until we are comfortable in the rest of the house." I don't think he had even visited the attic, or maybe he just took a quick look around. There was only one little light up there, and you couldn't see very well. I took my little flashlight with me to do some more exploring.

All kids like to discover secret hiding places, buried treasure, and such. You can only imagine how exciting it was for me anticipating a tour of Grandma's attic. Under the dust, I just knew there had to be all kinds of mysterious stuff. I had sorted through some Christmas decorations and old clothes when I found the trunk. It was hidden, way back behind dusty boxes that were filled with old magazines and books. I had hoped for a treasure trove of toys, or a horde of precious gems, or jewelry, or valuables. Instead, I found a trunk that was sitting there like it had been an original part of the house. Maybe the treasure was right here! There was a latch on the front where it might have been locked. But it wasn't. I pushed hard on the lid, and it popped open. It was too dark for my little flashlight to show the contents clearly, but they looked like just more old papers and books.

I sneaked quietly back down the stairs to get a bigger flashlight from the hall closet. When I returned and lit up the trunk, I began digging through dozens of old letters, diaries, newspaper clippings, and notes. Some of the letters were in bundles tied up with string, others were in little boxes with lids marked with dates, like 1809, 1836, and 1887. I knew these were from very old times, but I didn't think this old stuff had much value.

Suddenly, "Jacob, are you up there?" I heard Dad call out. I yelled back that I was. "What are you doing?" His voice was closer, so I just waited for him to reach me. "Look at this old trunk, Dad. Somebody has collected a bunch of really old letters and notes." Dad carefully inched past me and picked up a little box. "Shine the light over here," he said. The box was labeled 1809. He opened the lid and started leafing through the papers inside. "If you were looking for treasure in the attic, Jacob, I think you found it," he told me. I was relieved that I wasn't in trouble, but I doubted the suggestion that this was treasure.

After quickly examining a few more boxes in the trunk, Dad took the 1809 box and a diary and headed for the stairs. "Let's go down and show Mom and Liz," he announced. We turned off the light, and I lit the stairs with the flashlight as we descended to the dusty old bedroom.

Downstairs, we found Mom and Liz in the kitchen, putting the dinner dishes away. Mom was always insistent on cleaning up the kitchen after every meal. Come to think of it, Mom preferred everything to be as neat as her curly red hair. In a minute we were all back at the dining room table ready to examine the letters.

Dad briefly informed Mom and Liz of the trunk and then carefully lifted one page from the box and began to read:

> *June 24, 1809*
>
> *Dear Jacob,*
>
> *I know you must be wondering how a woman who is comfortable living in Philadelphia would be able to adjust to life on a farm in Adams county. When we first met, I sensed that you were somewhat hesitant to enter the social circle that was home to me. I can assure you of my intense and earnest desire to become a part of your world on the farm. Just writing this leaves me in truth quite whimsical.*
>
> *Please assure your parents and family members that I am ready and willing to embrace the tasks that farming life requires. I look forward to another visit with you later in the month when the rains abate and roads are passable.*
>
> *Mother and I have agreed that our wedding date would best be set for the coming November. It may be later, if you still have much to do on the farm. I will arrange for us to talk with my pastor in mid-October, if that is convenient for you.*
>
> *Love always,*
>
> *Maddie*

"Who is Maddie?" was my first question when Dad looked up from reading. Liz added, "Who was Jacob?" Dad thought for a moment. Then he told us that he did not know, but he guessed that the letters and everything in the box could be from some of our ancestors. How all this could have been preserved for more than a hundred years he had no idea. He thought that maybe there would be a clue among the papers in the trunk.

Mom had been quiet for a while. She looked like she was deep in thought. "I think we should sort through all the papers and check for names. Maybe we can uncover some Klund family names and do some research to find out more about these people. Surely there must be surnames on some of the papers."

Dad nodded his yes. "That is exactly what we need to do. It's a little late to start now, and we don't want to clutter up this or any other room in the house. I'm not doing much this Saturday. I'll set up the picnic table in the garage and we can bring the trunk down and start sorting everything that has dates, names of places, or people. I will ask some of the staff at the school where we can research genealogical information. I think this could be a fun family project."

Liz and I looked a little disappointed that we would have to wait, but Mom sensed our feelings and said, "The rest of the week will go by faster if you two get busy doing something. We will stop at the library after school tomorrow and check out a few books on early America. That may help us understand the letters better."

We visited Bethel Park Library and checked out *The History of Pennsylvania* by Charles Morris, a couple other early American history books, and a book on tracing family genealogy. I wasn't sure what that meant, but Dad anticipated my question. "It's about searching your family's roots; where great, great grandparents came from, who is related to you, and that kind of thing. We'll talk more about it after dinner tonight."

Before I take you any farther in this tale, let me share a little background on our family. I was born in 1947. Liz was the first baby, born in December of 1945. We were "baby boomers," born after Dad got home from the army near the end of World War II. Mom and Dad lived in Lewisburg, Pennsylvania when they got married. Our family moved into Grandma's house when I was just eleven, in the summer of 1958. As a youngster, I was immersed in the mystery of the old trunk in the attic, but it took some time for me to understand why the genealogy of our family mattered.

Now, twenty-two years after I discovered the trunk, I understand why this meant so much to Dad. He was born, Allen Klund, in New Providence, Pennsylvania in 1919. Mom was from Rochester, New York. They met when they were going to Bucknell University in 1939. That was in Lewistown. Dad was a history major and Mom studied biology.

Dad married Mom, Harriet McDonald, right after she graduated. He took a job teaching in Yeagertown that year. He didn't like it, so they decided to move to the Pittsburgh area. They found a little house to rent in Carlisle, and Dad taught high school there for a few years. That's where Liz and I were born and started school. We moved to Bethel Park and rented another house when I was in the second grade. Liz was in fourth.

Moving once again, to Grandma's house in Pleasant Hill, turned out to be a great idea. We hadn't been there more than a few weeks before we hoped to stay for a long time. It was sometimes sad to think about Grandma and Grandpa not being here anymore. I didn't really know Grandpa Klund. He died in his 50s when I was very young. I often stared at his photo on the fireplace mantel, trying to imagine his kind eyes looking down at me. Now Grandma was gone too, but we had many sweet memories of her in this house. Sweet meant much more than just Grandma's cookies. She was always calm, gentle, and loving.

We grew closer together as a family, just living in that house. And I began to realize that the contents of my grandparents' attic trunk would have a lasting effect on all of our lives. Now, twenty some years later, I still vividly remember those days when our family shared precious times reading those notes and letters.

We lived through the Cold War in the 1950s. The big threat was the Soviet Union and a new weapon, the nuclear bomb. That was frightening. If war broke out, whole cities could be wiped off the face of the earth. The thought of that haunted us, but remained mostly in the inner recesses of our minds. American families were strong, wages were rising, and television and the movies kept our minds off the perilous threat of a nuclear war.

I had not considered writing about life in the 1950s until now. But our country has been changing fast. The turbulent 60's and 70's changed many things in America—like our definition of freedom and our worldview. I sense that we need to refresh the memory of who we were—the foundational principles that tied us together. So, let's get back to the story. I will try to remember the details. I do have notes and Dad, as close by as the telephone, to get this right.

One Saturday in August, 1958, we awoke early. Mom was singing "The Twelfth of Never" and making pancakes. I think the smell is why Liz and I jumped up and bounded down the stairs. "No breakfast until you two are clean and dressed," she announced. Right back up we went. I returned to the kitchen in about two minutes. Liz took a while getting dressed, as usual.

As soon as we were seated around the table, Dad asked what we wanted to do today. I said, "I thought we were going to sort out the contents of the trunk."

"Right," he grinned, "just checking on whether you remembered and still wanted to do that."

We enjoyed the blueberry pancakes, but we didn't linger long at the table. Everyone's mind was on the trunk. Mom and I cleared the table, as Liz followed Dad out to the garage. I can still see us gathered together, ready to dig through the contents of the old trunk from Grandma's attic. Dad had set up the big picnic table right in the middle of the garage floor. The trunk lid was open and we could see the historic papers patiently waiting for us. The old trunk wasn't dusty anymore; and I thought it looked like a treasure chest.

Nobody moved or said anything. We just stared at each other for a few seconds. I think everyone knew that this was going to be an exciting adventure, but it was also a big undertaking. Reviewing all that stuff would take a long time. Finally, Dad spoke. "There is really no perfect way to do this. Maybe we should tape some labels on the table so we can put everything in chronological order. Liz, did you remember to bring the tape?" She did. Like Mom, Liz seemed to always remember what she was told to do. I could never compete with that. I knew that Liz was much smarter than I was, and she could make me feel small at times. But she also had Dad's quick wit and we usually got along well together. I knew that, in her heart, she really liked me.

Mom suggested, "We could just sit here and stare, or we could just dive in and try to make some order to all of it. After we get it in chronological order, we can make labels in twenty-year increments from the earliest to the latest papers."

Dad agreed that was a good way to start. So, he took four big stacks out of the trunk and placed one in front of each of us. "Look through your stack for the oldest date you can find, and try to get your pile in chronological order, oldest on top. We can make this fun. The person who comes up with the oldest pages will not have to do chores all next week. The other three will do everything. Fair enough?" Mom was the first to agree to that. Liz and I went along with the idea.

We began to sort through our stacks. "What if we can't find a date on something?" Liz wanted to know. Dad told us to put everything without a date in a pile in the center of the table. We got back to work. The only time we talked was when someone found an unusual item. But nobody wanted to let the others know the dates on their pages. Maybe a half hour or more went by. Then Mom told us she was finished. Mom was a fast reader; she offered to help me. Liz didn't complain. Instead, she just grinned, like she knew something we didn't know.

When Dad finished his stack, he helped Liz with hers. Then he told us "Ok, we will go around the table starting with Mom and report the earliest date you found."

"Here is a letter from someone named Harold to his mother dated 1836," Mom said, "but it can't be the oldest because we already read a letter dated 1809. I read a little of Harold's letter. He was living in Maryland. I think he had just moved there. I don't know where his mom lived because there is no envelope."

My oldest discovery was a copy of *Benjamin Franklin's Autobiography*. I thought he lived at the time of George Washington, but Dad opened the cover and found that the book was published in 1916. He said that was long after Franklin died, so it was probably a reprint. He decided that we could count my date as at the time of Franklin's death. Dad wasn't sure when that was, but he held up a little card he had found in his stack and told us it was a Revolutionary War Pension for a Sarah Schmidt dated 1790. "I think that would be just a little later than Franklin's death, so you might win, Jacob."

It was my sister Liz's turn. She had waited patiently, with a tiny grin every time one of us identified our find. "I think this is Barbara Holl Klund's diary, she said. "It's in another language, but it says right here, 1738. This must be the winner!" Dad took a look at the diary. He thought it was written in German. Yes, Liz had the oldest find from the trunk. We all congratulated her, but I wasn't very happy about having to do Liz's chore of helping wash the dinner dishes for a week.

We decided to take a break for a little while and resume our organizing of the trunk's contents after lunch. Mom told us we could either choose leftovers from Friday night's dinner or make ourselves a peanut butter and jelly sandwich. You can guess who chose the peanut butter and jelly. Mom and Dad ate some leftover spaghetti and meatballs.

When we returned to the garage, Dad reminded us we were stacking all of our papers, books, diaries, and other stuff in chronological order with the oldest on top. We would make as many piles as we needed. He said that anything without a date we would still keep stacked in the pile at the center of the table.

By the time we finished, most of the afternoon had slipped away. We were ready to do something else. Liz and I got on our bikes and took a little road trip. We were allowed on the county roads but not the state routes. Dad went out to the garage again to make a list of the trunk's contents. When Liz and I came back, he showed us his list and said it might just be one of the most impressive caches of historical materials any American family could ever find. I wanted to know what a "cache" was. He said it was a collection of similar things that had been stored or hidden away. I still have the list he showed us.

1. Barbara Holl Klund's 1738 diary

2. Johan Jacob's Klund's farm notes

3. Copy of a sermon by George Whitefield

4. Letter from a French and Indian War soldier

5. Excerpt from Thomas Paine's *Common Sense*

6. Letters from Johan Andrew and his son Frederick at Valley Forge

7. Hand-written essay on the Life of President George Washington

8. Pennsylvania Revolutionary War pension: Sarah Schmidt 1790

9. Letter from Maddie and wedding announcement of Jacob Klund and Maddie Drummond of Philadelphia in 1809

10. Catherine Berkhold's Diary 1812

11. Old Baltimore newspaper with lyrics to the Star-Spangled Banner

12. Harold Herman's letters 1836

13. Article about Charles Finney with notes

14. Albert Klund's family Bible and Civil War letters to his wife, Clara

15. John Ross and Anna Petit's wedding announcement and photos

16. Ledger signed by Andrew Carnegie

17. Old *Colliers* magazine dated 1901

18. Matthew Klund and Margaret Barr's son Peter's WWI letters home from France

19. Album of Matthew and Margaret's family photos

20. Peter Klund's World War I army discharge papers and letters to his family.

21. Twenty-three letters and notes with no dates.

When we had read through the list, Mom said "Lets drive into town and get an ice cream cone." "Yes!" That was the quickest response to anything that was said all day long. On the way into town, Dad thanked us for the hard work and he said he was excited about looking through everything we had found. Fortunately, we made it to Yeager's Ole Fashioned Creamery before it closed. On the way home, in between licks and slurps of ice cream, Mom asked Dad what we were going to do with all the things we had discovered. Dad said that we should talk about that and not make any quick decisions about what to keep or throw away. Mom thought we should keep almost everything because it was a part of Dad's family history. Dad agreed, and being a history teacher, he knew we could all learn something about our heritage from the letters, diaries, and notes. Liz and I enjoyed our ice cream in the back seat, thinking about the next bite more than their conversation.

When we turned in the driveway of the old house that we now called home, I saw it differently. Maybe this was where we could connect with our past, and that might be fun. We walked up the front porch steps, but before we opened the door, Dad turned to us and repeated his idea. "I think I would like for us to all spend some time learning about our roots and maybe some American history from the trunk. What do you all think?"

Mom spoke first. "I have never thought much about genealogy, although my brother, Cameron, likes to do it. I wouldn't mind looking through the old letters, if we could keep it fun and not make it a routine." Liz and I didn't say anything. We liked Mom's suggestion, but we weren't sure what Dad meant to do.

"How about once or twice a week, after dinner we read something from the trunk and talk about that instead of only sharing what we did that day?" Dad offered.

"Let's not commit to keeping it on a regular schedule. Maybe we would like to do it more often or less often. Let's just see where

it goes." That was Mom, never lacking in wisdom. I wholeheart-
edly agreed but didn't say anything. Liz seemed to be right with
me in that opinion because she also remained silent. I think we
all wanted to share some of Dad's enthusiasm for the project, but
maybe we were a little worried that he would take it too far.

I was glad for what Mom said. But, for me, the one really
great thing was that I was the one who had discovered the trunk.
Even Liz would have to admit that. I realized that I shouldn't gloat
about it, or Liz might lose her enthusiasm for the project. So, I
resolved to be humble to keep that from happening.

CHAPTER 2

Palatine Immigrants

MANY DAYS AFTER WE had sorted out the trunk cache, I wondered whether Dad had forgotten about the trunk. He hadn't. School had started, and he was teaching history at Bethel Park High School. That evening Mom was busy in the kitchen chopping up lettuce. Liz and I had settled in the living room with the tv on but doing a little homework.

I heard Dad come into the kitchen, and after a minute he greeted us before climbing the stairs, probably going up to change clothes. Shortly, he appeared again and winked at us. "I have some news. We haven't been able to talk about the trunk papers earlier this week because Barbara's diary was written in German. One of the high school teachers has been translating it for me. It's exciting. We can read a few pages after dinner."

"Does Mom know?" Liz asked.

"Yep," that's the first thing I told her when I came in," Dad reported. "Did you smell the pizza I brought home?" We hadn't, but we thought this was even better news than the diary.

We had nearly finished devouring the pizza and a salad when Dad started the genealogy conversation. He told us that with the help of another teacher and his Uncle Rudolph in Philadelphia, they had been able to trace the journey of Johan Jacob Klund and Barbara Holl from Germany to Philadelphia and then to Lancaster

County. There was plenty of information on German immigrants in the Pennsylvania State Archives. They even had passenger lists of arriving Europeans at the Port of Philadelphia dating all the way back to 1727.

Dad was excited to tell us that Johan Jacob Klund and his wife Barbara Holl with one son had arrived on the *Robert and Alice* on September 11, 1738. He told us that Barbara's parents and her brothers and sisters were among the several hundred immigrants from Germany to Pennsylvania that year. Dad said, "Barbara's diary fills in a lot of the blanks. So, who wants to read the pages that Mike translated for me?"

Liz volunteered. She took the papers, cleared her throat to focus our attention, and began:

July 10, 1738

The last few weeks have been very difficult. We had to pack our things and sneak away in the middle of the night. A few neighbors prayed for us before we left. We traveled more than a week to get to the city of Rotterdam. No one had much sleep. Ever since leaving the Palatinate, we have experienced fear, anxiety, hope, joy, and everything in between. It was so sad to leave friends in Bayern. Many tears flowed that night. Johan's parents were not healthy enough to risk the journey to the coast. I know that weighs heavily on his heart, even though his brother stayed behind to care for them.

Rotterdam is filled with migrants, mostly going to where we are, America. We could not even get close to the city. The noise, the jostling, the standing in line, have wearied me. Johan is strong, and he often lets me lean on his arm or lay my head on his shoulder. He says he needs me as much as I need him. I know he misses his parents. They have only a son and young daughter left at home now.

July 18

Finally, we are at sea. Rotterdam chose to rid itself of us. All of us are well, except little Andrew who is coughing. I am worried about him, and I am worried that this ship may not stay afloat to Dover. It is so crowded with people just like us, fleeing to a safer place. With good weather, Johan says we can be in port in two or three days. Several families gathered together this afternoon and prayed for that.

July 21

Dover. The winds have favored us. We could be boarding the Robert and Alice as early as tomorrow morning. It looks like a large enough ship to carry more than a hundred people. A man told Johan that Captain Goodman has made many trips across the Atlantic. That is of some comfort. Still, if I am a little weary now, I wonder how I will feel when we reach America. Our family gathered for prayer about the crossing again this evening. Father is a man of strong faith, and for that I am grateful.

Liz stopped reading and asked Mom if she would continue from here. Mom said Liz did really well, then she took the diary and continued reading:

August 1

A few days of calm seas and more good weather have raised my spirits. Andrew's cough has nearly stopped. We met a friendly family that Johan knows from his home town of Zweibruchen. They lost two sons in the wars. If only they had fled two years ago, they all would have been saved. I am so glad that, even though we lost our land, we made it away from the violence and hate that is spreading at home. I know it is not home anymore. It never will be.

August 22

The strong storms have finally passed. I am not sure how many more days it will take to reach Philadelphia. We must be at least half way. Johan and I have been praying for our family members every evening. Conditions on this ship are not good. There is little food. The smell of decay and human filth in our sleeping quarters is sickening. I am still recovering from the terrible rocking during the storms. They call it seasickness.

August 29

This week an illness swept through the entire ship. People are coughing, feeling chilled or feverish. Some have died and have been cast into the sea. Two were children. There is much weeping and sadness. We have just one doctor and he does not seem to know what to do. I worry about Andrew. Our family is praying for everyone and an end to this miserable journey. We don't know how much longer it will take. God help us all.

September 7

The captain says we will reach the port of Philadelphia in less than a week. We are tired but filled with hope. If we survive, how will America treat us? At least we have a place to go. Father knows a family near Philadelphia that has a large farm. We hope to exchange our family's work for food and a small house on their property. My father made these arrangements many months ago. We pray they are still willing.

Mom stopped reading. "I think there are some pages missing here."

Dad said this was a good place to stop because he had some details to add from his research. He told us that the Palatines were western Germans who emigrated in the 1700's because the French had invaded their land and destroyed their farms. After a terrible winter they were without enough food and firewood and they faced persecution for their Protestant faith. So, they contacted the Protestant community in Rotterdam and also Queen Anne in England for help. She permitted many to go to America. But they received no permission to emigrate from Germany, so a large number of them, including Johan Klund and the Holl family, had to escape in the middle of the night.

We talked for a while about how desperate these people had to be. Leaving their homes and going on the long and dangerous journey to America would have taken great courage, but they had little choice. We could not imagine these conditions. Our lives were so much easier. We all wanted to read more of the diary to find out how Johan and Barbara liked America, but Dad said it would take another day or two to get more pages translated from German to English.

A few days later, Dad told us that he had found out a little more about German immigration to Philadelphia in the early 1700s. He wanted to share something about that and about Benjamin Franklin. We nodded in agreement. Dad told us he found out that the Palatines who entered Dutch territory were not allowed to enter the city of Rotterdam, because the city feared they were carrying disease. They went to a holding area outside the city. There, an outbreak of an epidemic swept through the refugees, and the court asked the state of Holland to have them sent back to Germany or immediately on to America.

Johan and Barbara, with her family, boarded a ship for Dover, where Walter Goodman, the captain of the *Robert & Alice,* received them. Sometime, much later he sent a letter back to Germany, reporting that only 18 of his passengers died on the way to America. The other ships sailing in 1738 lost hundreds of passengers. There was so much pain and death that some called 1738 the Year of the Destroying Angels. This was a reference to the book of Exodus in the Bible when all the first-born children of the Egyptians died on the night Israel escaped from slavery.

Dad said, "Now here is what I found out about Ben Franklin. Many thousands of Germans were coming through the port of Philadelphia every year. So many, that the Provincial Council of Pennsylvania was alarmed that they would soon outnumber the English in the province. Benjamin Franklin was worried that German could become the official language of Pennsylvania. So, the Provincial Council created an oath of allegiance that male German immigrants 16 years of age and over would have to sign." He went on, "Before the women and children passengers could leave the ships in Philadelphia all male German passengers over 16 years of age were taken by small boats to authorities in the city. They had to sign papers agreeing to abide by the laws of the English government, to disavow allegiance to their former monarch, and to pledge allegiance to England."

I asked Dad whether Germans were moving into the other English colonies. He said yes, and then he explained the reason Germans were coming to Pennsylvania. William Penn had received a grant of land from King Charles II who owed his father, Sir William Penn, a large sum of money. The younger Penn was a Quaker who had experienced religious persecution. He decided to open up his colony to refugees regardless of their nationality or religion. No other colony matched Penn's acceptance of different nationalities and faiths.

We all understood that if it weren't for William Penn and Queen Ann we might not have been living here in Pennsylvania or even in America. I was beginning to realize that history matters, and I could hardly wait to hear what happened to Johann and Barbara in their new homeland.

The next week, Dad came home with more translated diary pages. We could tell he was really getting into this genealogy thing. He did wait until we were nearly finished eating before launching into his findings. "I was curious about a few things, but I think the diary helps quite a bit," he began. "Did everything go well at the Port of Philadelphia? Were Barbara and Johann married? Where would they find a home?" The rest of us were asking ourselves the same questions. "Here are the next several translated pages. It seems that only a page or two are missing. Who will read?"

I volunteered and read,

September 14

Philadelphia

Johan, my father, and my brother were taken off the ship to sign some papers. They finally returned. We had been waiting and worrying for several hours. Father said he was sorry but it took longer than usual because he did not have complete immigration papers. He had tried to explain that we had little time to prepare because of the dangers we faced. Just then a man in the street saw father and recognized him. He pushed through the lines and approached the desk. "I know this man's family," he said. "They are from Bayern, where I used to live. Good people." The agent asked the man his name. It was Conrad Schneider, who had lived less than two kilometers from us in Bayern. The agent asked Mr. Schneider if he would sign some papers. He did, and the agent said if the men would sign their oaths we were free to go.

September 21

Lancaster

Mr. Schneider helped us find a wagon and driver who brought us here to the Schmidt farm. They had already been building a little house for all of us, but for several days we have been sharing the Schmidt's house. Father, Johan, and James are working hard to complete our building, but they also have to spend a few hours every day helping with the harvest. So much to do. This is a busy place.

September 29

Our house is nearly completed. I found time to talk with Mrs. Schmidt about meeting with the pastor of their church and introducing us to his congregation. We need to get to know people in our area and Andrew should be going to school and learning English. Johan and I would like to learn some English also, but we can't afford a tutor.

I paused in my reading and asked if someone else wanted to finish. Dad said that this was probably a good place to stop. He said he thought Johan Klund and Barbara Holl were married because they had a child. Barbara Holl was the name used on the ship manifest, probably because her family came with her. Dad asked whether anyone had a question or a comment. Liz wanted to know whether the Schmidt family spoke German or English. Dad didn't know, but he thought that if they had lived in America for a few years they might know English. It would be useful for selling their crops and doing other business in town. But he said it was not likely that they spoke much English at home.

Lia said, "So, we are Germans, right?

Mom answered, "You are part German and some other nationalities. I am Irish, Scotch, and English." She paused and then said, "Who are the Pennsylvania Dutch?"

Dad nodded. Being a history teacher, he knew a lot about that kind of thing. "The word for German is spelled D-e-u-t-s-c-h and pronounced *Doitch*. In spite of the fact that it doesn't quite sound like Dutch, some people believed that these were Dutch folk. Many people still call it Pennsylvania Dutch country over there, but my folks were really German," he grinned.

"Hey Dad, it's Friday night. Could we go into town for some Pennsylvania Dutch ice cream?" Liz teased. We were all for it. I winked my thanks to Liz in the back seat of the car.

The next week we read through many more pages of Barbara Holl's diary and found a little newspaper clipping noting the newcomers, Johann J. Klund and the Holl family, to the Moravian Church of Lancaster, Pennsylvania. It said that there would be a lunch on the grounds to welcome them next Sunday.

"There are just a few diary pages beyond this one," Dad observed. "Perhaps raising a family took up too much of Barbara's time." I guessed we would just have to imagine how their lives went. Dad looked at me for a couple seconds and then told us that there were other papers dated after 1738 and we would be looking at them next week.

Dad looked like he had more to say, but he hesitated. Mom said, "What is on your mind now?"

Dad answered, "I wonder whether we will ever find out who put all that stuff in the trunk, who passed it down from generation to generation, and why Grandma never said anything about it. This is a mystery that I hope something in the trunk may help us solve." We all hoped he was right.

At our usual family sharing time the following day, Liz spoke up. She said that some of the girls in her class at school were making fun of her freckles. They started calling her "freckle face," until one girl called her "spotty the potty cat." Then several other girls joined in. She didn't know what to do about it.

Mom offered a little encouragement and advice. She said that her own freckles were part of what attracted Dad to her and she told Liz that at her age girls are trying so hard to be accepted by their peers. They may all flock together around someone who acts strong, partly out of fear of being left out. The way to overcome that is to be strong yourself. "Liz, you are beautiful, smart, and kind. Just be yourself and ignore the name-calling. All this will pass. In fact, there will probably be many girls who will take courage from you. We will pray about that." Before we left the table, we did.

CHAPTER 3

Breaking Away

JUST BEFORE WE TURNED the calendar to November, Dad brought the rest of Barbara Klund's diary back from school. There were only a few pages left to read. They began several years later, in 1752. For some reason, Barbara had stopped writing in her diary for several years. Dad said he wasn't sure why or whether we should read these last pages because . . . He stopped, but then he decided to go ahead. "By this time the Klunds had two more children, Matthew and Sarah. Matthew was probably a teenager."

Mom took the diary and began to read the diary:

> *October 15*
>
> *Yesterday Mr. Schmidt asked Matthew to take the wagon out to the field to gather shocks of wheat. The day was cool and dry. Matthew asked me if he could take his sister along with him. Sarah loved to ride in the wagon. She is only seven, and I knew she would not be much help, but I said she could go if her brother would be careful. Matthew said he would.*
>
> *In a little while Luke Schmidt ran into our house without knocking. He said Sarah fell off the wagon, and she was hurt. We hurried out to the field. Matthew was kneeling down beside her. Sarah was groaning and her leg looked like it could be broken. We picked her up and carried her*

to the house. I asked Luke to hurry and ride into town to find a doctor.

After two hours the doctor came. He was an old bearded man with deep wrinkles around his eyes. I took him to Sarah, lying in her bed. He felt the leg and said that it definitely was broken but he could reset it. He asked the two of us to hold Sarah still. She had stopped crying, but when he pushed the bone back into place, Sarah screamed and I took hold of her hand and cried with her for a long time.

Mom paused in her reading. We knew that, as a mother, she was feeling the pain that Sarah had to endure, even though it was a long time ago. We quietly waited for her to resume. In a minute or so she said "I will go ahead with the story."

The doctor fixed a splint on her leg and told me not to let her walk on it. He will come back in a month to see how it is healing. Matthew looked so sad. I know he believes the accident was his fault. I told him not to feel so guilty; accidents can happen to anyone. But I felt guilty too for letting her go on the wagon.

Mom stopped reading, and Dad told us that anesthetics for pain were rare in those days. Sometimes people just bit down on a piece of wood or a lead bullet while surgery was going on. It hurt me just to think about that, and I could see by the expression on Liz's face that it bothered her too.

There were only two more pages written in the diary. They didn't mention what happened to Sarah. We hoped we would find out as we read through other letters and notes.

On the final two pages of her diary, Barbara wrote about Johan negotiating to purchase some land of their own. Dad said that he had made a call to Lancaster County for old property records and found that Johan Klund bought an 80-acre farm in 1754. Even though it was a long time ago, we were happy for their family.

The next Saturday evening, our family returned to the Klund history. Dad said that before we read more papers from the trunk we probably should know something about the American colonies. He started by telling us that the Germans in Lancaster

County were Christians—church-going people, but by the early 1700s England and her colonies had drifted far from their devout ancestors. In England, gin was the popular drink and drunkenness spread throughout the land. Public hangings were a frequent form of entertainment. In America, Africans, who were at first indentured, became permanent slaves. Dueling was often used to settle arguments. On both sides of the Atlantic, church attendance declined, and the clergy no longer talked about a personal relationship with God.

Dad continued, "Despite the power of these evils, a big change was coming. In 1739 a young minister, John Wesley, began preaching in England. Because he spoke about the need for personal salvation, he was not welcome in the Anglican Church. So, he held his meetings in open fields. Thousands of people came out to hear him. Some jeered and threw stones, but Wesley continued to preach a simple call to repentance. More and more people attended his meetings. His brother, Charles, began writing hymns. Many of them we know today, like 'Hark the Herald Angels Sing,' and 'O for a Thousand Tongues.' People began to call the Wesley brothers Methodists because of their methodic practice of daily devotions. A major spiritual awakening broke out in England."

"The revival spread to America. A powerful speaker from England, George Whitefield, came to preach in the colonies." Dad told us his name is pronounced "Witfield," although it is spelled Whitefield. His open-air sermons sometimes reached as many as 15,000 people at a time. One of those people was Ben Franklin, who became Whitefield's publisher and friend. Whitefield's publications alone doubled the output of the American colonial presses. Dad read what *Ben Franklin's Autobiography* had to say about the preacher who was about to become his friend.

> *I happened . . . to attend one of his Sermons, in the Course of which I perceived he intended to finish with a Collection, and I silently resolved he should get nothing from me. I had in my Pocket a Handful of Copper Money, three or four silver Dollars, and five Pistoles [Spanish coins] in Gold. As he proceeded I began to soften, and concluded to*

give the Coppers. Another Stroke of his Oratory made me asham'd of that, and determin'd me to give the Silver; and he finish'd so admirably, that I emptied my Pocket wholly into the Collector's Dish, Gold and all.

"Was Whitefield getting rich from those collections?" Liz wanted to know. Dad told us that Whitefield wasn't raising money for himself; he needed money to build a children's orphanage in Georgia. And he had something else on his mind. In 1752 he wrote to Franklin, "As you have made a pretty considerable progress in the mysteries of electricity, I would now humbly recommend to your diligent unprejudiced pursuit and study the mystery of the new-birth." Franklin considered Whitefield an honorable and devout preacher, but he backed away from the personal salvation message.

Dad continued, "America had its own noted evangelists. One was Jonathan Edwards, who delivered a strong warning in a sermon called 'Sinners in the Hands of an Angry God' to his congregation in Northampton, Massachusetts. Edwards and other evangelists called for a return to repentance and a personal salvation. That marks the beginning of a movement known as the Great Awakening. Its followers broke away from the traditional churches and formed what they called 'new light' congregations. This awakening came on the eve of the American Revolution. The new churches were the main supporters of petitions, protests, and calls for independence from Britain. When the Revolution broke out, they became the Patriots, while most Anglicans remained loyal to the king."

Dad looked at his watch. He said we all have chores to do, so we had better stop for now. He told us that before we talked about the American Revolution at our next meeting we would read a letter from the French and Indian War. Liz asked why the French were fighting the Indians. I wondered the same thing. Dad said the name of that war is a little misleading. If we could wait a few days, he would tell us about it.

On Sunday morning Mom said she felt sick. She had a headache and upset stomach. Maybe a little fever. Dad suggested that we stay home from church and take care of her, but Mom told us to go. She said she just needed to get some rest. So, we got ready and went to church. I asked my Sunday School teacher to pray for Mom. On the way home, Liz told me she did the same.

We left church quickly and Dad drove the Chevy fast. I could tell he was anxious to find out how Mom was doing. When we came into the house, Mom was upstairs sleeping. Dad told us to be quiet and make ourselves peanut butter and jelly sandwiches for lunch, then do some reading or go and play outside. We decided to ride our bikes to the Murphy's. We played Monopoly with Ted and Jane all afternoon.

Mom was feeling much better by Tuesday. She even made chicken and dumplings for dinner. Nobody made dumplings as well as Mom. After dinner we were ready to hear about the French and Indian War.

Dad remembered Liz's question about the French fighting the Indians. He said, "The French were friendly allies of the Indians, especially in the Ohio territory. They were trading their goods for furs. The French didn't want the English colonies spreading into their territory. As the English settlers moved west, they came into contact with French troops and Indian braves. With French guns, Indians began to raid the frontier settlements."

"Virginia claimed to own all the land west of the Ohio River. So, Governor Dinwiddie ordered a 22-year-old lieutenant colonel, George Washington, to build a chain of forts along the river to keep the French out. But when Washington's men arrived in Western Pennsylvania, they found that the French were already there. Washington marched his men a few more miles and built a fort called Necessity not far from the French Fort Duquesne. Then his troops met and skirmished with a small band of Frenchmen, killing their leader, Coulon de Jumonville, and nine others."

"The French retaliated, capturing Washington at his fort in July of 1754. They let him and his men go after he signed a surrender document that mentioned their killing Jumonville. This started what we call the French and Indian War. When he returned to Virginia, the governor demoted the young Washington, but George refused to accept the rank of captain and resigned his commission."

Dad paused briefly, long enough for Mom to ask a question. "I didn't know that Washington dropped out of the militia. How did he get back into the military?" Apparently, Dad had been refreshing his memory on this. He told us that the year after Washington resigned, the British named him senior American aide to General Edward Braddock. Then they sent Braddock on another expedition to capture Fort Duquesne and expel the French from the Ohio Country.

"I have a letter that was in the trunk. It was written by a Jacob Nicholas Holl, who was on the same ship that brought Johan Klund to America. He must have been Barbara's younger brother. He wrote:

Dear Barbara,

The march with General Braddock through Maryland into western Pennsylvania was tiring. Even though he was old and slow as a turtle on his feet, I liked the general. We were not far from the French fort, Duquesne, when we were suddenly attacked by a large force of French and Indians. For a few minutes we held our own, but caught in a crossfire, our troops began to panic and flee. General Braddock tried to rally them, but he was shot off his horse and killed. All would have been lost except for a young aid to the general named George Washington. He took charge of the retreat. We buried Braddock in the road and ran the wagon tracks over it so that the Indians could not find him and desecrate the body. We are safe now, making our way back through Maryland. It is good to be alive. I hope to see you in a few months. Greet Johan and your sisters for me.

J. Nicholas

Dad told us that during this skirmish Washington himself had two horses shot from under him and his hat and coat were pierced by several bullets. Now we know that the Indians ceased firing on him because they believed he could not be killed. As a result of his bravery, young George regained his reputation as a leader.

Years later Washington is said to have met the chief who had fought against him in the Pennsylvania woods. The chief said, "You will become the chief of nations, and a people yet unborn will hail you as the founder of a mighty empire. I am come to pay homage to the man who is the particular favorite of Heaven, and who can never die in battle."

Dad continued, "In 1763 the British won the war with France. With French military units removed from the frontier, the colonists were expecting to be able to expand westward. But King George III did not want to spend money defending the frontier against Indian attacks, so he issued the Royal Proclamation of 1763. It stopped the westward expansion of all thirteen colonies. This restriction was just one of the many decisions of the king and Parliament that led to the American Revolution."

I was so caught up in Dad's stories that I didn't want him to stop, but he thought this was a good place to quit because two of us had school in the morning, and Mom probably needed to go to bed early. "Do you have any papers from the trunk on the American Revolution?" Liz wanted to know.

Dad smiled with that little twinkle in his eye that told us he had something special for us. He said yes, but it would take some time for his friend to translate some more letters that were written by one of our ancestors. We might have to wait until after Thanksgiving to find out what was in these letters.

On Wednesday we had a delicious dinner of sauerkraut and pork with mashed potatoes. Grandma had taught Mom how to make it years ago. To top off the meal, Mom baked a big apple pie. We were all stuffed. Maybe we were preparing ourselves for Thanksgiving.

Liz and I sat quietly as Dad read a verse from scripture. "I am the resurrection and the life; he that believeth in me, though he were dead, yet shall he live." Dad said that Jesus spoke these words to Martha just before he raised her brother, Lazarus, from the dead. "Christians throughout history have embraced this promise of a resurrection. It sustained the apostle Paul and thousands of martyrs in the Roman Empire, and I think it was the source of faith for many during the American Revolution." He said we would talk about that tomorrow.

I asked Mom and Dad whether Grandma was dead or still living somewhere else. Mom explained, "Grandma's spirit is alive and with God right now. That's what Christians believe. And Jesus taught that there will be a physical resurrection someday, so she will have a new body that will never die." I felt better, because I really wanted to see Grandma and taste another one of her peanut butter cookies.

On Friday Dad came home with more letters translated. Liz and I hurried to finish our homework before dinner so that we could have lots of time to talk after we ate. Dad seemed to be in a hurry to get started too. He finished eating first and began.

"You probably know a little about the American Revolution, but what I have here should make it more real to you. Before we read these letters, we need to take a quick look at the causes and early history of the Revolution. The French and Indian War created a huge debt for the British government. So, the British Parliament passed a series of taxes on the colonies. Nobody likes taxes, especially if they are imposed without a vote of the people."

"The colonists were furious, and protests broke out against taxes like the Stamp Act. The Tea Act also brought a strong reaction. Bostonians refused to buy English tea. The ships could not unload it. Then a band of colonists calling themselves the Sons of Liberty, dressed up like Indians, boarded the ships, and threw chests of tea into the harbor. When the British punished Boston by closing its port, other colonies sent food and supplies overland to the city."

"Tension in Boston led to a confrontation in which a soldier shot five citizens. Colonists called it the Boston Massacre. The people of Massachusetts began to store weapons and ammunition. You may know that the fighting started at Lexington and Concord where British troops were sent to seize the weapons. So, fighting had already broken our when colonial leaders met in Philadelphia and signed a Declaration of Independence."

"The men who signed the Declaration were risking their lives and the lives of their families. They were considered traitors. King George of England had the power to torture and hang them and their families. He was furious. That's why the last line of that treasonous document declaring independence read, 'And for the support of this Declaration, with a firm reliance on the protection of Divine Providence, we mutually pledge to each other our Lives, our Fortunes, and our sacred Honor.' We will find out how much that pledge cost them next tune, maybe Saturday."

That concluded our evening conversation. I had read a little about the American Revolution at school, but Dad seemed to know much more than our textbook. On Saturday evening, Dad returned to the Revolution, "I forgot some of what we were talking about, so last night I did a little research. Seventeen of the signers fought in the American Revolution. The British captured five of them during the war. Richard Stockton of New Jersey never recovered from his incarceration. He died in 1781. Two of Abraham Clark's sons were captured by the British. Eleven signers had their homes destroyed. John Hart died while fleeing after the British destroyed his mill."

Dad was right, the war cost all of them much hardship. We all shared what we thought freedom meant to the colonists. Then Dad said he didn't have the next letters he wanted us to read translated yet. He did have a clipping from a very famous defender of the Revolution, Thomas Paine. He said that most American soldiers knew who that was and read his writings. Then he read this to us from *Common Sense*:

> *Europe is too thickly planted with kingdoms to be long at peace, and whenever a war breaks out between England and any foreign power, the trade of America goes to ruin, because of her connection with Britain. The next war may not turn out like the last, and should it not, the advocates for reconciliation now will be wishing for separation then, because, neutrality in that case, would be a safer convoy*

than a man of war. Every thing that is right or natural pleads for separation. The blood of the slain, the weeping voice of nature cries, 'Tis time to part. Even the distance at which the Almighty hath placed England and America, is a strong and natural proof, that the authority of the one, over the other, was never the design of Heaven. The time likewise at which the continent was discovered, adds weight to the argument, and the manner in which it was peopled encreases the force of it. The reformation was preceded by the discovery of America, as if the Almighty graciously meant to open a sanctuary to the persecuted in future years, when home should afford neither friendship nor safety.

Dad explained that the roots of many long-held American attitudes can be found in this writing. One is the belief that the United States should not be entangled in Europe's affairs. Another is that the Atlantic Ocean was a good protection from aggressive countries that served us for more than a hundred years. Finally, Paine was convinced that God wanted America to be a refuge for persecuted people and a sanctuary for religious freedom.

We talked a little more about what the founders believed. Dad said Jefferson, who wrote the Declaration of Independence, had inserted a line or two about ending the evil slave trade. The delegates removed that and some of his other ideas. Ben Franklin tried to console Jefferson over the deletions. Slavery would survive through the Revolution, but some slaves would win their freedom by serving in the military.

Dad promised us that he was having more translating done. We would wait to return to the usual family sharing time until after Thanksgiving. Evenings were getting longer because it was late November and it got dark soon after dinner. Our church had already begun to prepare for Christmas, so we went to practice for the program on Saturday afternoons. As we neared the holidays, we skipped family sharing time to work on decorating the house. Dad and I worked outside; Mom and Liz did the interior.

Thanksgiving finally arrived. We usually had some family members join us for the feast. This year Mom's parents came. Liz and I loved Grandpa and Grandma McDonald. We didn't get to see them very often because they lived in Rochester, New York. But they always sent presents for Christmas and birthdays. Grandpa was almost as funny as Dad. His thick white hair looked like snow.

Mom was very excited to have her parents with us, and she worked long hours in the kitchen on Wednesday getting food prepared. The turkey went into the oven about the time they arrived. We sat and talked for more than an hour before Dad brought up the subject of the trunk. Grandpa seemed really interested in that. Grandma went out to the kitchen to help Mom.

Dad showed Grandpa MacDonald some of the treasures from the trunk. They read a few diary pages together. Grandpa said he thought much of the trunk's contents were very valuable, and he suggested that Dad consult with an expert about that. The evening passed so quickly. Mom had asked me to let Grandma and Grandpa sleep in my bedroom, so I took a blanket downstairs to sleep on the couch. They did have to climb the stairs, but it didn't seem to bother them.

On Friday all six of us packed into our car and took a drive so the MacDonald's could see the area where we lived. They really liked being out in the country. On Saturday morning our grandparents were ready to go back home. Their visit was too short. I can remember standing in our driveway waving goodbye with a sad feeling in my whole body.

That evening after dinner, Liz said she wanted to tell us something about the girls who were teasing her. We were all anxious to know the latest development. Liz looked at Mom and said, "Well, I tried to do what you told me. I just walked away when they started. It didn't help, because they were having too much fun calling me names. But one of the girls, Cassidy Taylor, came to up me as we were leaving school. She said she didn't want to be part of that group anymore and she offered to walk away with me the next time it happened. Sure enough, the next day Cassidy went to lunch with me. When the mean girls started in, Cassidy and I just ignored them. Then Elaine and Marilyn walked away from their group. That was it. They all quit the name calling. I guess it wasn't fun anymore.

Mom said she was glad Liz shared that with us, and she was relieved to hear that it worked out as it did. Dad told Liz he was proud of her and of all of us for praying about it. Mostly, we were just happy for Liz.

CHAPTER 4

A Time for War

ONE AFTERNOON, JUST TWO weeks before Christmas break, Dad came home from school with a big grin. "I have in my ink-smeared hands a whole bundle of letters and the translated pages we have been waiting for," he informed us. Mom's chicken and noodles were great, but nobody took their time eating. We were really getting into this genealogy thing.

"Do you know about Patrick Henry?" Dad asked. We assumed he was going to tell us, so we waited. He explained that when the British closed the port of Boston the other colonies increased their support for Massachusetts. Patrick Henry was a Virginia delegate to the Continental Congress where he proclaimed "The distinctions between Virginians, Pennsylvanians, New Yorkers and New Englanders are no more. I am not a Virginian; I am an American." After the first battle at Lexington and Concord on April 19, 1775, Henry stood up in Virginia's House of Burgesses and gave one of the most dramatic speeches in history. He raised his voice and swung his arms as he spoke. Here is how he concluded.

> *"Our petitions have been slighted, our remonstrances have produced additional violence and insult; our supplications have been disregarded; and we have been spurned, with contempt, from the foot of the throne . . . we must fight! I repeat it, sir, we must fight! An appeal to arms and to*

the God of Hosts is all that is left us! The war is actually begun! The next gale that sweeps from the north will bring to our ears the clash of resounding arms! Our brethren are already in the field! Why stand we here idle? What is it that gentlemen wish? What would they have? Is life so dear, or peace so sweet, as to be purchased at the price of chains and slavery? Forbid it, Almighty God! I know not what course others may take; but for me, give me liberty or give me death!"

Dad added, "On that last line, Henry pounded his chest with an imaginary dagger. The drama must have been intense."

"Changes were coming fast. On June 16th the British attacked the American position on Breeds Hill outside Boston. They captured the hill but lost many British troops at what we call the Battle of Bunker Hill. The next day the Continental Congress in Philadelphia appointed George Washington to lead the American army. Washington hurried off to Boston. There, a standoff between the British and Patriots lasted until March of the following year when Washington was able to seize Dorchester Heights, overlooking the city. Henry Knox dragged canon that he had captured at Fort Ticonderoga to Washington's men, who pulled them up the hill. When the British saw the American guns facing down on Boston they decided to leave for New York."

"Washington then decided to leave Boston and try to trap the British troops on Long Island, New York. That was a big mistake. He was greatly outnumbered and could have lost his entire army but for some miraculous weather. Washington's men were able to construct fortifications on Brooklyn Heights, because a heavy downpour prevented a British attack. His troops were split between Manhattan and Long Island, and British ships controlled the surrounding waterways. They could easily have cut off Washington's escape."

"The Americans were in a dangerous position, but a northeast wind swept in and prevented the British ships from sailing. Then heavy rain and an unusual shift in the wind opened a path for the Americans' retreat. They escaped in small row boats across the

East River to Manhattan. At midnight the wind ceased for an hour, then a gentle southeast breeze allowed bigger sailboats to speed the evacuation, and most of the army was swiftly deposited in Manhattan. Some soldiers were still in danger, but a dense fog rose out of the wet ground and continued to linger after the sun came up blocking the British view until the American troops were safely ashore. Many people still consider this evacuation a miracle."

"Now, are we ready to read the letters that I promised?" Dad was being a little overly dramatic. Of course, we all agreed. "Ok, these letters and notes are from Johan and Barbara's son, Andrew, who was in the Continental Army off and on throughout most of the war. And Andrew's son, Fredrick, was also at Valley Forge. I have here a letter from Andrew, who served during the winter of 1776, when Washington crossed the Delaware River into New Jersey. Many people think this daring move saved the Revolution. The coincidence is that we are going to read this just before Christmas, and that's the season of the year when this letter was written."

Dad continued, "Do you remember Andrew, Johan and Barbara's son? He came to America, worked on the farm, and then joined Washington's army. His letter was written in German, probably because his parents preferred it to English. Still, the translation makes it as if we are right there. Here, Jacob, you read it." I accepted the paper and read:

> Dear mother and father,
>
> Five days ago, General Washington decided we would attack the Hessians in New Jersey. We were losing enlisted men every day, and the general seemed desperate. Someone told me that Dr. Rush saw a paper on his floor that said "Victory or Death." Our daring plan called for every move to be covered in secrecy. We broke camp and marched east. On Christmas Eve, just before we were to cross the Delaware River, they read this from Thomas Paine to us: 'These are the times that try men's souls, the summer soldier and the sunshine patriot will, in this crisis, shrink from the service of his country; but he that stands it now deserves the love and thanks of man and woman. Tyranny, like hell, is

not easily conquered; yet we have this consolation with us, that the harder the conflict, the more glorious the triumph.'

Those were powerful words, but we were a poor and weak army. On our march, I saw tracks of blood in the snow from those who had worn out their shoes. We arrived at the river while an icy wind was blowing and boarded big black boats that had been used for hauling iron ore. Huge chunks of ice floated all around us. It got colder and began to snow. The heavy canon couldn't get across until long after midnight. We reached the muddy shore and marched half frozen in total silence with only moonlight. We were several hours behind schedule, and General Washington was very agitated. With all the marching there was plenty of time to think. Can I trust the general? Are we marching into a trap? Will I freeze with fear when they begin shooting?

With all of our problems, we still surprised the Hessians. When our canon rolled into the streets of Trenton, many of them surrendered. We were tired from marching, but we fought hard against the Hessians who had not fled. Their captain was shot and killed. It was a great relief and celebration when we took hundreds captive. We were so weary but victory was sweet, I really believe God was with us.

Our army captured many guns, supplies, and horses. The boats carried us back across the freezing river. Some of us had to walk part way on the ice. But I am in camp now, and a fire is burning. I miss you.

Merry Christmas to all

Andrew

I handed Dad the translation and he paused to see whether we had any questions. I asked who the Hessians were. Dad told us that they were paid soldiers from Germany, hired by Britain. "So, they were here just to make money?" Mom wanted to know. "Yep, that's about it," Dad said.

"Are there other letters from Andrew," Liz asked. Dad said yes there were, but he thought we had spent enough time on the

Revolution tonight. He suggested we wait to do the next letter after the holidays. That was fine with me. I looked forward to Christmas visits from some of my aunts and uncles with their kids. That would make Christmas really fun.

Three days before Christmas we began our break from school. Dad took us out to a tree farm, and we cut down a tall spruce. Mom and Liz helped decorate it. That was the year I got my first baseball glove. It was for a lefty. We were too far away from a Little League, but Dad said he would play catch and let me hit a ball in our back yard, which was really big. But I had to promise to help cut the grass beginning in the spring. I asked if I could invite some of my friends to play ball in the yard. Dad said we could but not to hit the ball toward the house. That made a lot of sense.

Grandma and Grampa MacDonald didn't come for Christmas that year because he was suffering from the flu. We had just the four of us for opening presents. No relatives arrived, so we invited the pastor's family to visit for dinner on Christmas day. They had two kids who were a couple of years younger than I was, but all four of us had fun outside building a snow man.

Uncle Bryce and Aunt Lucy Fisher came the day after Christmas. Lucy is Mom's sister. Two of their children came with them. Paul and Janice were a few years older than Liz. We asked them where William was. They told us that he went to his girlfriend's house in Harrisburg. They were students at Penn State. Still, we had great fun. We played a couple of new games that they brought along. That evening it snowed enough for us to throw snowballs at each other.

The following day, the Fishers left after lunch. Dad said we could get back to the American Revolution that evening, After dinner and before reading another letter, Dad told us that Washington's troops lost several battles in 1777. He was unable to defend Philadelphia. When the British took the city, the Continental Congress that was managing the war fled west to Lancaster, Pennsylvania. In December, Washington marched his sick, tired, cold, and hungry army to Valley Forge, about 20 miles from Philadelphia.

That is where Andrew was when he wrote this letter. "Now, who wants to read?" Liz reached out for the next translation and read:

Dear Betsy,

We marched many miles to this camp, leaving another trail of blood in the snow because some men have no shoes. In spite of the cold, we are living in tents while we build cabins. This is surely a mixed army. Most speak English, but the rest of us speak German, French, Dutch, or even Polish. Some of the men will be going home in the next few days, where I hope they recover from this misery. As you know, I will stay through the winter. We are mostly eating fire cakes. They are just a mixture of flour and water. I heard that most of the farmers around us are trying to sell their crops to the British in Philadelphia for a goodly sum. I know they have to feed their families, but it troubles our men and the general that they are helping the enemy.

Many men in this camp are sick and some are dying. We have almost no meat. Perhaps you could ask a few of your farmer friends, and neighbors whether they could send us a small wagon with food, especially a little meat. Fredrick could bring it, if you think he is old enough. He is strong and healthy. Also, a blanket or two would be very good, if you can spare one.

I believe General Washington could win this war if we had support from the Congress or most of the people. I must go. There is a roll call to see how many men are still in camp. I love you. Tell my folks I am ok.

Andrew

Liz handed the letter back to Dad, who said, "There is no date on that letter, but we know that the army entered Valley Forge in December of 1777. They camped there so that they were out of easy reach of the British but close enough to keep watch on the enemy. To me it is amazing that these men continued to believe in the possibility of winning the war. The situation seemed desperate. This next letter is probably from several weeks later. Would you read it, Jacob?" I took it and read:

My Dear Betsy,

Thank you for your prayers and help. Fredrick arrived here safely yesterday. He is such a strong youngster. We have been eating a little better, and what you sent is a big help. Some of the fellows told me to send their personal thanks. Frederick is going to stay a while, so the blankets will keep us warm. The weather has not been so cold this week.

Counting those who died, mostly from disease, and those whose terms were completed, we have about half of the army we had when we first encamped here. I do have some good news. Baron von Steuben, a military officer from Prussia, has joined us. Gen. Washington believes that he will make a big difference in our training. He is tough but fair. The drilling is long and hard, but now we have more food. As we get stronger, hope seems to be rising in the camp. It is good having Frederick here. He has already made friends with several young men about his age. Some of them are good with the fife and drum. Fredrick is learning to beat the drum. He seems to be improving fast. Our spirits are not nearly as low as they were a month ago. Keep us in your prayers. I miss you very much.

Andrew

Dad took the translated page and added, "Young boys, even pre-teens, were in Washington's army. Some went with their fathers, others enlisted to help earn money for their families in those desperate times. Many learned to play the fife or drum. Fifes and drums were used to announce the daily activities. They signaled when the troops would get up in the morning and retire at night, even when to eat. They called men to assemble, and sometimes sounded an alarm. They used special notes and beats that the troops understood."

Dad said that the war went on for another four years. Just before Washington's men entered Valley Forge, Americans under General Gates defeated British General Burgoyne at Saratoga, New York. Benedict Arnold was a hero of that battle. He later became a traitor. But the most important result of Saratoga was that King

Louis XVI of France was impressed enough with the American victory to formally join in the fight against their old enemy. The Americans alliance with France may have been the turning point in the war. They provided funds, some good leaders, and a navy. We had one more letter from Andrew, but Dad wanted to save it for another day.

Mom spoke up, "We can take a little more time for just one letter. What is it about?"

Dad said it was about Yorktown, the last battle of the Revolution. Andrew must have gone home for a couple of years, then re-enlisted. Many men did that. Washington was never sure how many soldiers he could count on. But the longer the war went on, the better chance the Patriots had of success. The British needed this rebellion to end.

"Ok," Mom said, "Let's leave all that drama for another day. It will be good to have some family sharing time until Saturday. Then we will have plenty of time to talk." That's what we agreed to do.

When New Year's Day arrived, the snow came down fast and furious. The county roads were closed. I was not happy that the snow had come too soon. By the time school should start, the plows would have cleared the roads. We watched several college football bowl games. The most exciting was Syracuse beating Texas in the Cotton Bowl. Even Mom enjoyed that one, because Syracuse is in New York, her home state. We enjoyed three more days before school resumed. January often seemed the longest month of the year, even though the days were shorter. At least we got to sleep in on Saturday mornings.

So, on the first Saturday evening of January, we returned to the American Revolution. "Let me set the stage for this letter," Dad said. "The South was deeply divided between Patriots and Loyalists. The Loyalists were mainly people who were not affected much by British policies. Some worked for the government as tax collectors, some were wealthy merchants, others were Anglican ministers or Quakers who did not believe in fighting. The Loyalists, who made twenty to thirty percent of the colonists, believed they were better off under the mother country. The British relied on these people, and they tried to divide the Southern plantation owners from the backcountry farmers. They also encouraged slaves to escape, offering them freedom for joining their side."

"The last year of the war was fought mostly in the South. When British troops captured Charleston, South Carolina, things looked pretty dark for the Continentals. It could have been worse. Benedict Arnold defected to the other side and almost succeeded in turning over West Point to the British."

"There was one positive note in the South. Francis Marion, of South Carolina, often called the 'swamp fox,' harassed the British, continually attacking and then retreating into the heavily wooded marshes. Lord Cornwallis, with a large British army, had moved into the western hills, but he turned toward the coast when he ran out of supplies and needed fresh troops. His destination was the little village of Yorktown, Virginia. George Washington's army was 500 miles to the north, and he was planning to attack New York. The rest of the story is in this letter. Here Mom, read it for us."

September 28, 1781

Dear family,

I hope you are well. I am fine. I am more than fine. For this reason: early this month, I think about the 5th, General Washington revealed a secret plan to us. He would try to trick the British into thinking we were going north to free New York. But we would move south through Virginia. Here is how he did it. He sent a letter to the French General Lafayette, describing a plan to march into New York. It was not in code and he knew it would be easily intercepted by a British patrol. What we found out later was that Lafayette, Washington, and French General Rochambeau were planning to trap the British in Virginia. We had spies among the British, so our generals knew that under General Cornwallis they were moving toward the coast to meet ships with supplies. Lafayette asked for assistance from a French fleet in the West Indies. Comte de Grasse with his fleet responded by turning north.

Lord Cornwallis moved his entire army toward Yorktown. We had been five hundred miles north of him, but we marched south nearly 20 miles each day, mostly at night. The French fleet sailed north in time to block British ships from reaching Yorktown with supplies. A big naval battle broke out in the Chesapeake Bay. When we set up our siege line around Yorktown, it was obvious to Cornwallis that he was trapped. He and his entire army surrendered. They came forward and laid down their arms. It is a sight I will never forget. We celebrated as our band played "The World Turned Upside Down." I saw many tears of joy. I believe the war could be over. Thank you for your prayers. Tell Betsy that I expect to come home soon.

J. Andrew

When Mom looked up from her reading, Liz asked "Was the war over?" Dad told us that there was a little fighting after that, and the peace treaty wasn't signed until two years later, 1783.

"So, does anyone have some thoughts to share?" Dad asked.

Mom spoke first. She talked about the hardships that the colonists endured for more than six years. Then she said she had been thinking about the unlikely events, maybe miracles, that seemed to come at precisely the right time. I asked whether she was thinking about the weather that saved most of Washington's army on Long Island. She did believe that was really a miracle. "So was Trenton, Saratoga, and Yorktown. Washington prayed a lot, didn't he?" she said.

Dad affirmed that and added that Washington was a godly man, and he had even recorded the date of his spiritual conversion in his diary. But he was human and had faults like all of us. He lost his temper and often got discouraged.

Liz broke in, "He also owned slaves, didn't he?"

"Yes, he did," Dad agreed. "I thought that we might be talking about this, so I did a little research. He owned slaves, but it is a little more complicated than whether he did or didn't. He was born into a society that had owned slaves for a hundred years. Washington inherited some slaves when he was only 11 years old. When he married, his wife had many more from her deceased husband. He didn't consider it wrong until the time of the Revolution."

Dad said he had read that one of the neighbors thought Washington was a stern boss on his plantation. He also had a gentle side. He really cared about his slaves' well-being. Another neighbor reported that Washington treated his slaves better that anyone in the area. And by the time of the Revolution, Washington had begun to believe slavery was wrong. His conversations with Lafayette helped change his mind. Washington said, "I can only say that there is not a man living who wishes more sincerely than I do, to see a plan adopted for the abolition of it."

Dad explained that Washington thought a gradual elimination of the system was best because freeing so many at once would be disruptive and create hardships for many freed people who would have no place to go. There were 317 enslaved Africans living at Mount Vernon. Less than half, (123) were owned by George Washington. He freed all of those in his will when he died. But his wife, Martha, had 153 dower slaves from Daniel Custis, her former husband's estate. By law she could not free them and they reverted to the Custis estate.

Dad wrapped up the discussion. "Knowing that Washington owned slaves causes many people in our time to judge him negatively. But, when he died, the American people made him a great hero. He would not have liked that. Maybe be his best quality was humility."

Our sharing time was finished, and Mom reminded Liz and me that we had some chores, but she let us take a break to play Monopoly. The evening went by quickly. I was tired and ready for bed. It had been a big day. The next morning, I told Dad that I had dreamed I was a drummer in the Revolution. He winked and said, "I'm glad you survived." That's how Dad is, always trying to be funny.

We were still laughing when Mom broke in. "Speaking of surviving, do you remember that we all wondered whether Sarah Klund survived after she broke her knee? She was on the Schmidt farm and fell off the wagon."

We did remember, and Dad said he thought that the first trunk papers we sorted out mentioned a Sarah Schmidt. Liz was thinking hard. "She must have married one of the Schmidt brothers whose parents owned the farm in Lancaster County," she said. "I wonder if it was Luke, who reported that Sarah fell off the wagon?" We all agreed that it would have been a good story.

Dad was already on his way to the closet to pull out something from the list. "Here it is. Look here, the Revolutionary War Pension that Pennsylvania gave to Sarah Schmidt in 1790. It's hard to read the handwriting, but there is the signature of Governor Thomas Mifflin." Dad showed us the paper. Mom studied the handwriting for a while and discovered that Sarah was a nurse in the war. We were all satisfied to know that Sarah had lived a long life.

After reading what Dad called "original sources" on the American Revolution, we paused again in our genealogy and history discussions. I was glad to get back to family sharing time. The winter was snowy, but not too cold. January was going by fast. I remember bringing home my report card that year. There was a big "A" in the box under *History*. I knew It was partly because of a report I wrote on the French and Indian War. Mom thought our family discussions were a big help to me. I agreed.

Mom paused for a moment, probably to reflect on how to tell us what she was about to say. "I have to ask you kids for a little help," she said. "For a few months I thought that I could handle working three days a week and still manage the house. But I can't give both of these the proper attention, and I don't want to quit working at the park. This spring, I wonder if you could each take on one or two more chores?"

We could tell that she really didn't want to have to ask for help. So, without any hesitation we both said, "Sure." Then Liz asked Mom what it was that we could do.

Mom smiled and told us thanks for being agreeing to help. Then she said that there were several things that we could do, but she would give us a choice and we could each pick one. She needed someone to sweep the carpets and floors, someone to sweep or hose off the front porch, someone to dust and polish the furniture, and everyone to put their dirty clothes in the laundry instead of dropping them on the bedroom floor.

Oops! We knew we were guilty of that last one. "Ok, Liz said, "I can pick up my clothes, and I would choose to dust and polish the furniture once each week."

Mom said that would be great and then looked at me. I had a choice of sweeping the porch or the carpets. I thought about it a minute and then told Mom I would do both the porch and the carpets. She was very happy to accept my offer. And Dad told us that he was proud of us for taking on another chore. He said we could celebrate it this weekend at a restaurant. We chose Sandinis.

For the rest of the week our sharing time was based on Matthew chapter five, the Beatitudes. Dad wanted to talk about "blessed are the meek," He said that "meek" does not mean weak. It doesn't mean that you should not stand up for what is right, or to be tough. It means being gentle, humble, and have self-control. Jesus is the best example. He was not proud, and he was easy to approach, but he challenged those who were in power and doing wrong.

Then he told us that he was concerned about the direction the Supreme Court might take regarding freedom of religion. He did not want to get involved in the politics of that, but he felt he might need to take a stand in some way. He asked us to pray about it. We said we would.

Everybody was busy the next week. We had just a few minutes for family time after dinner. Liz and I had lots of homework. Dad was grading papers. Mom had some paperwork from the park. Finally, on Friday night we celebrated finishing the week with dinner at Sandini's. They had a big menu, but Liz and I ordered hamburgers.

When we came home, Dad wanted to talk about history. He told us that during the American Revolution, the Continental Congress proposed a form of union for all the states. They called it the Articles of Confederation. Four years later, all the States had ratified the document. It resolved the people's greatest fear—the power of a central government like Britain had. Under the Articles, each State kept most of its governing power. Each State was equal and had one vote in Congress. It required a two-thirds majority vote to pass anything.

Fighting the British had united the country. But not long after the war ended, division set in. States began to act independently from each other. The national government had no power to deal with inflation or falling farm and business income. There was no national system of printing money. Congress had no power to force the states to help pay the war debt. So, several leaders met at Mt. Vernon and Annapolis to talk about these issues. They called for all the States to send delegates to Philadelphia in 1787 to revise the Articles. All the States, except Rhode Island responded.

During the long hot summer, the delegates wrote an entirely new document, the Constitution. It was cobbled together with many compromises. Each State would be represented equally in the Senate with two senators. The more populated states would control the House of Representatives. The States retained some powers and delegated to the United States other limited powers. That is called the Division of Powers. The national government was divided into three branches; the legislative to pass the laws; the executive, to enforce the laws; and the judicial, to handle cases arising under the laws. That is called the Balance of Powers.

Dad said, "After all the debating, the divisions, and the compromises, Ben Franklin rose to speak. He was old, but respected." Dad read part of Franklin's his final speech to the delegates.

> . . . I consent, Sir, to this Constitution because I expect no better, and because I am not sure, that it is not the best. The opinions I have had of its errors, I sacrifice to the public good. I have never whispered a syllable of them abroad. Within these walls they were born, and here they shall die. If every one of us in returning to our Constituents were to report the objections he has had to it, and endeavor to gain partizans in support of them, we might prevent its being generally received . . . . I hope therefore that for our own sakes as a part of the people, and for the sake of posterity, we shall act heartily and unanimously in recommending this Constitution.

All the States ratified the Constitution by 1789. In the meantime, George Washington was unanimously elected president. In fact, many people voted for the new Constitution because they assumed that he would be the president. Many other people hesitated to give their approval to the Constitution unless it added a Bill of Rights, additional protections against a powerful central government. The memory of harsh British rule still lingered in their minds.

Dad said, "One of the most important things to remember about the Bill of Rights is that they simply limit the government from removing your rights. The Founders believed that every American has rights endowed by God. The amendments were passed to protect these rights from a repressive government.

"At the time the Americans rebelled, England had an official, government endorsed church, the Anglican church. Other religious groups were persecuted. So, the Founders added the First Amendment with this opening statement, *Congress shall make no law respecting the establishment of religion nor prohibiting the free exercise thereof.*"

"So, we have freedom of religion. Congress cannot establish a religious group. Nor can Congress prevent you from doing so. This is not a protection for what you believe. No government can take that away. It is religious expression that is protected. You can talk about, write about, and exercise religious beliefs in many ways, in every public place, or wherever freedom of speech is protected."

"This is what the Founders believed when they wrote the Constitution. It is not what everyone believes today. The Supreme Court may decide to limit religious expression by state or local government employees in their places of work. That would be a major change in the interpretation of the First Amendment. A major irony is that the oak doors of the courtroom where the Supreme Court judges sit have the Ten Commandments engraved on them. I think that qualifies as religious expression."

Dad said, any questions? Silence. Mom said, "I think we got it."

For the next few weeks we had family sharing after dinner. One evening I brought up something that had been on my mind for weeks. I asked Dad and Mom if we could have a dog. I could tell that they weren't ready for that question by the long pause. Finally, Mom said, "Why do you want a dog, Jacob?"

I was ready for that question. "Most of our friends have dogs, and they really have a lot of fun with them. We are way out here in the country, and a dog would give us something to do.

Dad wasn't convinced. "Well, you know on most days during the school year no one is home until evening. When we do get home, there's a lot to do. I have papers to grade, Mom has dinner to make, you have homework. I don't see where there is much time to take care of a dog." I had to agree with those points, and I didn't argue about it. But I still wanted a dog.

The next evening, we returned to the family history. Dad told us that the American Revolution was only the first fight for freedom. The threat returned in 1812 and that's what it is called, the War of 1812. We were fighting the British again because they didn't respect our sovereignty or independence. They refused to surrender the western forts as they had promised in the Treaty of Paris that ended the Revolution. They also stopped our ships at sea and forced Americans to serve in their navy. Their excuse was that they were looking for British deserters. And they interrupted our trade with France, because they were at war with France again.

"How did that happen?" I asked.

"Well," Dad answered, "It's a little complicated. The French royal treasury was bankrupt from its wars, including the American Revolution. When the government tried to increase taxes, France had a revolution and overthrew the king. But their revolution got out of control. Radicals seized the government, and the violence became so intense that the military stepped in and took over. The military under Napoleon Bonaparte set out to build a French empire, encouraging uprisings across Europe."

"The little general, Napoleon, defeated Spain, and he placed his brother on the throne. In 1803, Thomas Jefferson saw this as an opportunity to expand the United States and control the port or

New Orleans. He offered to purchase the city from France. They offered to sell the whole Louisiana Territory. We paid only fifteen million dollars for it and doubled the size of our country."

"England, a long-time rival, responded to the French threat. Their navy tried to blockade French ports. Sometimes British sailors defected to an American ship. So, British warships often stopped and searched American merchant vessels for defectors. They seized many naturalized American citizens in a policy called impressment."

"When Congress declared war on Britain in 1812, we could not guess how much trouble it would cause. In 1814 the British captured Washington D.C. President Madison and government officials fled. The president's wife, Dolly Madison, stayed and took charge of saving government documents and fled before they burned the president's house. It's called the White House today because it was painted white to cover the black smoke and stains left after the British set it on fire. That was in August. The next month British ships approached Baltimore, Maryland. A big naval battle in Chesapeake Bay was followed by a bombardment of Fort McHenry."

"An American, Francis Scott Key, had witnessed the burning of the Capitol and other public buildings in Washington. He was trying to obtain the release of a local doctor that the British had taken prisoner and held on their ship. Officers on the British flagship agreed to the release, but they put the two Americans on a small vessel under armed guard until the battle was over. Key watched the attack through the night on the deck of that ship and jotted down a poem he titled 'instead of "The Defence of Fort McHenry."'

"We have a copy of it in page of a Baltimore newspaper dated September 27, 1814. You will recognize the poem when Liz reads it." He carefully handed the paper to Liz and she read,

> Tune: Anacron in Heaven
> O! say can you see by the dawn's early light,
> What so proudly we hailed, at the twilight's

last gleaming,
Whose broad stripes and bright stars through
The perilous fight,
O'er the ramparts we watched, were so
gallantly streaming.
And the Rockets' red glare, the Bombs bursting
in air,
Gave proof through the night that our Flag
was still there.
O' say does that star spangled Banner
yet wave,
O're the land of the free and the home
of the brave?
On the shore, dimly seen through the mists of the deep,
Where the foe's haughty host in
dread silence reposes,
What is that which the breeze,
o'er the towering steep,
As it fitfully blows, half conceals,
half discloses?
Now it catches the gleam of the morning's
first beam,
In full glory reflected now shines in the stream:
'Tis the star-spangled banner!
Oh long may it wave
O'er the land of the free and the home
of the brave!

And where is that band who so vauntingly swore
That the havoc of war and the
battle's confusion,
A home and a country should leave us no more!
Their blood has washed out their
foul footsteps' pollution.

No refuge could save the hireling and slave
From the terror of flight, or the
gloom of the grave:
And the star-spangled banner in triumph doth wave
O'er the land of the free and the home
of the Brave.

O thus be it ever when freemen shall stand
Between their lov'd homes and the
war's desolation!
Blest with vict'ry and peace may the heav'n
rescued land
Praise the power that hath made and preserv'd
us a nation!
Then conquer we must, when our cause it is just,
And this be our motto – "In God is our trust,"
And the star-spangled banner in triumph
shall wave
O'er the land of the free and the home
of the brave.

When Liz handed the newspaper back, I admitted that I didn't know there were other verses. Dad assured me that many people do not know that either. Then Mom asked who the "hireling and slave" were in that verse about "their foul footsteps." The historian in Dad came out. He said there is no dispute about the hirelings; they were the Hessians and British soldiers and sailors who fought for the king only for the money. The slaves may have been American slaves who sided with the British. In the American Revolution and the War of 1812; the British promised them freedom if they joined their army, and many did. But some scholars believe that the slaves were the same as the hirelings from Europe.

We talked a little about the slavery problem, and Dad said we would probably find out more when we get into the Civil War era. This was a good stopping point, but we all decided that we should get right back into the discussion tomorrow.

After dinner the next evening, Dad told us that he wondered why a Baltimore newspaper would be among the papers in the trunk. That is until he read a little of Catharen Klund's diary. It was the next item from the trunk. He opened the diary and turned several pages to where he wanted to read about the War of 1812. He said this is something that happened in Maryland during that war. Harold and Catherine Klund lived there. Catherine wrote these diary notes,

May 5, 1813

We just learned that the British have burned Havre de Grace. The local militia was outnumbered and overwhelmed. Many townspeople fled and are homeless. We may be asked to take in a family if this happens closer to Queenstown.

May 13, 1813

Samuel Prichard stopped by this morning to warn us that the British were within a day's march of Queenstown. Harold and the militia could be called to duty any day. The men are meeting on the green in the evening. We talked about where to go, if the British come here.

May 15

Harold's militia met this morning, on news that the British were approaching Queenstown. This afternoon they moved toward the oncoming troops just outside town. Shots were fired, but the British backed away, for now. I know we are in danger. Maybe we will have to flee.

May 22

Harold met together with four farming families at doctor Rhineheart's house. They are worried that whatever they plant this year could be seized by the British. The men finally decided that they cannot fail to plant because it is their only source of income. We will just have to accept what happens and pray.

June 2

So far, we are safe, but a few towns in the counties north of us have felt the British fury. They seized food and people's personal belongings, then they burned their houses. Harry and Major William Nicholson's militia are preparing for the worst.

July 4

Queenstown had its annual celebration of independence today. It wasn't as festive as it usually is. We are all worried, because the British army is so close to us. Major Nicholson told us the plan for evacuation, if we are attacked. I haven't seen Harold all week.

Aug. 10

British forces are in our county, approaching Blakeford. I have begun to pack our clothes and whatever we can pile into our wagon. I tried to calm the children's fears, but I am at least as fearful as they are. The militia gathered on the green today. Harry came home and stayed last night. I felt more secure with him at home.

Aug. 13

The militia has held off the British at Blakeford, and we hear that the town is safe. Our men are still scouting British movements. They could move toward Queenstown at any time. I believe we are prepared to flee. But I hope Harry is here when we do.

Aug. 14

The 35th and 38th militia companies were called in to defend Slippery Hill. The British arrived yesterday and the battle continued into the evening. They couldn't hold the town, and families that fled are entering Queenstown. We are probably next in line for a British attack. I have loaded the wagon with everything we can take. Harold is still with the militia.

Aug. 18

Our worst fears have been realized. About 300 or more British moved from Slippery Hill toward Queenstown.

Fighting broke out along the Queenstown Road. I have taken the wagon with the children and left town going south. We prayed for Harry and the militia, but the British took the town. I heard that the militia has withdrawn to Centreville. We have no home.

Aug. 28

The British are still encamped at Queenstown. I heard that they ransacked the Bowlingly estate. The family will be devastated. We stopped to rest near a farm. The owner asked us where we were going. I told him that I did not know, and he invited us to stay. We feel safe now at the Wright's house. They have been so kind to me and the children. I am worried about Harry if the British attack Centreville.

Sept. 28

We heard that the British had left Queenstown a week ago, so we thanked the Wrights and said good bye. I hitched up the horses, and we took the road back toward home. We didn't know whether the British had destroyed our house. We traveled for hours, and thank God, the house was still there. It was in terrible shape. I have to redd up the whole place and clean everything because British soldiers used it for a month.

Sept. 29

Harry returned. We are blessed. He can get some rest and reopen the store, but the British are still a threat. Baltimore has been attacked. Harry brought a newspaper from the city. It has helped us understand what is happening across the state. I liked the poem about the defence of Ft. McHenry. I wonder who wrote it.

"That was a lot of reading," Dad said, "but now we can understand the hardship faced by everyday people when a foreign nation invades. Thankfully, we haven't had that happen since 1814. And, by the way, the reason we have the Baltimore paper is that Harold and Catherine Klund lived in Maryland at the time. We need to preserve the paper and probably most other papers from the trunk, not only because they mean a lot to us, but because they could be valuable."

Mom said she was impressed by the way Catherine took charge of loading the wagon and moving their belongings. It must have been really frightening, knowing the British army was so close and having no plan for where to flee. Dolly Madison also seemed to have a lot of courage packing up government documents and preserving important papers before fleeing the capital.

Dad agreed. He told us the Treaty of Ghent that ended the war was approved by the British Parliament in December of 1814. Neither side won anything. The news of the treaty didn't reach the United States for one month. During that month, Americans from Tennessee and Kentucky under Andrew Jackson defeated the British who were attacking New Orleans. So, maybe the main result of the war in America was that Andrew Jackson became a hero and would later become president. One more thing, The U.S. and Britain have never fought each other again.

CHAPTER 5

One Nation

I AWOKE TO THE smell of pancakes. Oh, it was so good to be wakened by the sweet aroma from Mom's kitchen. I dressed quickly and descended the stairs. Liz and Dad were already at the table. "You slept in," Liz teased. I asked what time it was.

Mom said, "It's nine o'clock, but that's ok. You have been working very hard, and I thought it would be nice to treat you to your favorite breakfast. We didn't have any blueberries though. Sorry." We all chimed in that her pancakes were the best, blueberries or not.

That evening we returned to our usual family sharing time. Most of the talk was about what happened at school and at work that day, but we did read chapters from the Gospel of Matthew. It was kind of strange reading about the birth of Jesus in the middle of February. It would have fit better into Christmas.

When Herod tried to kill Joseph's and Mary's baby, they fled to Egypt. Reading that part of the story reminded me of Catherine Klund's packing up a wagon and leaving home to get away from the British. I wondered why God would have allowed Herod to kill all the babies under two years old. Or why wars have to happen. So, I asked about that.

Mom said that was a great question. Then she explained that many scholars and writers have written about this issue. "Here's how we understand it," she said. "Remember Adam and Eve? They had a perfect life, but they disobeyed God. The Bible calls that sin. Sin is the result of our own personal choices to disobey God. He does not prevent us from making choices. He wants us to love Him and be obedient, but that is our own decision. The scripture gives us plenty of information about how we should live. When we ignore or reject the commandments, especially to love God and our neighbors, bad things usually happen. Selfishness and hatred are evidence of our sinful nature. Wars are one of the worst consequences, but there are many other ways we hurt other people every day. Lying, cheating, pride, and greed can all lead to trouble, sometimes even war."

Mom continued, "Remember when some of the girls in Liz's class were calling her names? God didn't come down and stop it. But we prayed and found a way to deal with it. And Liz learned an important lesson on how to handle that kind of thing. So, yes, we all have choices, and things work out better when we follow what the greatest teacher of all time says. We all know who that was—born in Bethlehem, dedicated in Jerusalem, raised in Egypt, crucified in Jerusalem, alive in Heaven."

February arrived right on time and the best thing about that for me was getting a day off for President Washington's birthday. I was glad that I knew a little about him, and I thought he deserved the honor of a holiday. That night I told Dad that it would be fun to visit Mount Vernon. He just nodded.

When we returned to the trunk papers, Dad thought we should to talk about one of the worst evils in history—slavery. He explained how it came to America. The Spanish brought the first Africans as slaves on the islands of the Caribbean Sea. More African slaves were brought to Central and South America than to the British colonies in North America. But there was still a significant number in the British colonies.

Dad explained how the British colonies began using Africans as indentured servants. "Remember when Johan Klund and the Holl family came to Pennsylvania? They were too poor to buy a farm, so they agreed to work on the Schmidt's farm in exchange for a place to live. That's called an indenture. The contract usually lasted from four to seven years. And, because land was so cheap, indentures often received a piece of land when their time was fulfilled. Some even received livestock and clothing."

"The first Africans sold in Jamestown, Virginia were also indentures. After a certain period of time, they were free. All their children and future generations were free. But, later there was a great demand for labor, and some states changed the law to make African indentures permanent. That is slavery. After that, anyone born a slave was a slave for life. After the invention of the cotton gin, slavery provided labor that made large plantation owners very wealthy. Slavery was an institution that was not going to be easy to change."

"How long did slavery last?" Liz wanted to know.

Dad said, "Slavery ended in Britain before it did here. Over there a young Christian politician, William Wilberforce, spoke out against it. He and his friends started an antislavery campaign and gathered a million signatures on petitions against slavery and delivered them to the House of Commons. Wilberforce and four other members of the Clapham Sect of Christian activists worked tirelessly until Parliament passed the Emancipation Act in 1833 only three days before Wilberforce died."

"Here in the American colonies, there were some early voices against slavery. The Quakers opposed it and several of the founders spoke out against it. You remember we talked about George Washington changing his mind on that. Thomas Jefferson wanted to see slavery end, too. He authorized a proposal to abolish slavery to the Virginia legislature in 1778. Delegates to the First Continental Congress in 1774 pledged to stop the importation of slaves to America. Almost all the northern states had abolished slavery before 1800."

"The anti-slavery movement got a big boost from an evangelist. Charles Finney was a young lawyer in New York during the early 1800s. But he quit his law practice after a powerful religious conversion. Finney became a great revival preacher, drawing huge crowds. One of his converts, Theodore Weld, moved with him to

Ohio when Finney was invited to be the president of Oberlin College in 1835. There the students, along with Finney and Weld, came to believe that slavery was a sin. Oberlin was the first American college to accept women and African Americans as students. One of our ancestors saved a copy of a Finney sermon on the subject. It is long, but I want us to read a few lines. Who will do it?" Mom said she would.

> *"Do you ask, What ought Christian men to do? Doubtless they ought to use all their legitimate influence against the Fugitive Slave Bill, and against all the political aggressions of slavery upon our free land and government. Doubtless they ought to vote for freedom as against slavery, and speak out in no mistakable words and tones, till the nation shall hear and shall purge itself from all national patronage of this horrible system. When I entered the ministry, not a word was said about the relations of the American Board to slavery, or of the Bible Society, or the Tract Society. But ere long the question came up in regard to the relations sustained by each of those societies to slavery. The Christian public ask, What is the true position which those societies sustain towards slavery? . . . They should consider that increased light begets augmented responsibilities, and that they cannot pass along now, treating slavery as if it were no sin—however conveniently they might have done so in those times of ignorance which God winked at. There is too much light now on the sin of slavery, and on its multiform relations to the church and to the nation, to admit of neutrality in regard to it, or to allow the assumption that it is not to be regarded as a great sin.*

When Mom finished reading, Dad explained that Lyman Beecher, the father of Harriet Beecher Stowe, joined the anti-slavery movement. Their house in Cincinnati, Ohio was a station on the "underground railroad," a secret way to smuggle slaves through the North into Canada. Harriet probably heard a ton of stories from the people they hid. Later she wrote *Uncle Tom's Cabin*, a book that exposed the terrible consequences of slavery to both the slave and the master. The book swept the nation and greatly increased anti-slavery sentiments in the north.

From the 1820s on, Congress was divided over slavery. The nation was growing, adding new states in the West. Northern states were opposed to the spread of slavery. Southern states wanted it to spread into all of the West. When Missouri became a state, Congress passed a Compromise that split the territory in the West along a line of latitude. Slavery would be permitted south of the line. Free States would be formed north of it. This proved to be just a temporary fix to the slavery issue.

Stephen Douglas, a Democrat senator from Illinois, proposed the idea of popular sovereignty, meaning the people in each territory could choose by their vote for or against slavery in each new state. Dad said, "It sounds fair doesn't it? But it didn't work well at all. Slaveholders and anti-slavery people poured into Kansas before the vote. A civil war broke out in that territory."

Dad continued, "As new states prepared to join the Union, slavery was always an issue. The West was developing fast. I have to interrupt the division over slavery for a few minutes, because we have a letter from a branch of the Klunds that you will like. Not all the Klunds stayed in Pennsylvania. In fact, many of them joined the westward movement that was expanding the country before the Civil War. Did you ever hear of the Oregon Trail?"

Liz thought she had, but she wasn't sure.

So, Dad went on, "President Polk was an expansionist. He wanted to fulfill the American destiny to extend from the Atlantic to the Pacific. While he was in office, the United States added Texas, Oregon, and California. The Oregon Territory included what is now the State of Washington. American missionaries went to Oregon to convert the Indians. And by the time they realized the Indians were not much interested in converting, American settlers were arriving in large numbers. The fertile soil and mild climate attracted them."

"There were no roads across the West or through the Rocky Mountains. But hunters, known as mountain men, became guides through the mountain passes. Wagon trains crossed the prairies and climbed the mountains, often with great peril. One of the Klund's and his family reached Oregon. We have an account of it that probably was sent back to a Klund relative in Pennsylvania. I believe it could have been Harold Herman, but it is more likely Albert, because it was in his Bible. I just found it. Here Jacob, I think you will like to read some of this." I did.

September 19, 1846

"Dear family,

We have been in Oregon since August, but I didn't have time to send you an account until we were settled in, housed, and became part of the community. You may know something of the Oregon Trail from the newspapers. They treat it as if it is an adventure. The truth is that it was an ordeal.

We set out from Independence, Missouri in a party of some fifty wagons. We were very organized, with by-laws and rules to govern us. We even elected officers. They decided that we would always be moving by seven in the morning. With stops for eating we could average about fifteen miles a day. We always circled the wagons for safety before sundown. Sunday mornings were reserved for rest and religious meetings. We stopped at springs and streams to clean clothes and fill our barrels.

Our family soon found out that we were overpacked. The oxen were getting tired from the heavy loads, so we had to leave heavy stuff like furniture and anything we didn't really need along the trail. The routine of packing and unpacking, walking beside the animals, enduring the hot sun, high winds, and thunderstorms made us weary. Some people couldn't bear it, and did stupid or dangerous things, like lying down and refusing to move, or shooting their rifles at shadows.

We faced high winds and barely survived a tornado in Kansas. It is very flat out there, and you can see for miles. We were frightened to see a tornado dip from the sky and come toward us. We had nowhere to hide. About a half mile from us, it lifted back up into the clouds. I have not heard so many loud prayers as we said that day.

The wagon train had to pass through Cheyenne territory and were very worried that the Indians would attack us. A band of them did approach, but they just observed us for a while and then turned away. We should have worried more about the mountains and the weather. A bad dust storm kept us pinned down for more than a day, and it took another day to get clean enough to move again.

Swollen streams in the Rockies were a big danger. We lost four wagons and several people while we tried to cross a stream after a thunderstorm. The guides should have been more careful. Ten more people died from an illness that we could not name. High fever, no appetite, red blotches on their skin. We thanked God when we finally arrived here. It took more than a week to feel normal again. This is a beautiful place, but I call the journey the Oregon Trial.

Give my love to all,

Joel Klund

I handed the letter back to dad. "Wow, you read the whole thing!" he said.

"Yah, Dad I learned how to read in school," I admitted. Mom laughed and told me I was turning into Dad.

Dad resumed his history lesson. "As new states like Oregon entered the Union, the issue of slavery became intense, The Republican Party emerged as an organization opposed to the spread of slavery into the West. With the deep division on this issue, a crisis was inevitable. Presidential candidate, Abraham Lincoln, predicted it in what is called the "House Divided" speech. I had a copy of it in my files. Here is a short excerpt from it.

Mr. President and Gentlemen of the Convention.

If we could first know where we are, and whither we are tending, we could then better judge what to do, and how to do it. We are now far into the fifth year, since a policy was initiated, with the avowed object, and confident promise, of putting an end to slavery agitation. Under the operation of that policy, that agitation has not only, not ceased, but has constantly augmented.

In my opinion, it will not cease, until a crisis shall have been reached, and passed. "A house divided against itself cannot stand." I believe this government cannot endure, permanently half slave and half free. I do not expect the Union to be dissolved — I do not expect the house to fall — but I do expect it will cease to be divided. It will become all one thing or all the other.

Either the opponents of slavery, will arrest the further spread of it, and place it where the public mind shall rest in the belief that it is in the course of ultimate extinction; or its advocates will push it forward, till it shall become alike lawful in all the States, old as well as new — North as well as South.

Dad explained, "When Lincoln became the Republican candidate for president in 1860, the nation was on the verge of splitting. When he won, the southern states began to secede from the Union. He was faced with doing whatever it would take to restore the Union."

"There is some controversy over Lincoln's words about slavery. He often spoke out strongly against it. But in a letter to Horace Greeley during the Civil War he said, 'If I could save the Union without freeing *any* slave I would do it, and if I could save it by freeing *all* the slaves I would do it; and if I could save it by freeing some and leaving others alone I would also do that.'

"Some people think that this shows that Lincoln didn't mind if slavery continued. Nothing could be farther from the truth. His main concern was the preservation of the Union, but he often spoke against slavery. Here are a few Lincoln quotes:"

You know I dislike slavery; and you fully admit the abstract wrong of it.

—August 24, 1855 in a letter to Joshua Speed

I have always hated slavery, I think as much as any Abolitionist.

—July 10, 1858 in a speech at Chicago

As I would not be a slave, so I would not be a master. This expresses my idea of democracy. Whatever differs from this, to the extent of the difference, is no democracy. August, 1858

We know, Southern men declare that their slaves are better off than hired laborers amongst us! . . . There is no permanent class of hired laborers amongst us . . . Free labor has the inspiration of hope; pure slavery has no hope. September, 1859

In giving freedom to the slave, we assure freedom to the free — honorable alike in what we give, and what we preserve. We shall nobly save, or meanly lose, the last best, hope of earth.

—December 1, 1862 a message to Congress

Dad paused and Mom said, "I think you made your point about Lincoln's beliefs. But you are preaching to the choir."

I wondered what that meant. Liz did too, because she said, "What is preaching to the choir?"

Mom explained, "It means the listeners already agree with what you are trying to convince them about, like the choir usually agrees with the preacher in church."

Dad couldn't miss the opportunity to be funny. He said, "So I guess we will end choir practice for tonight. Thank you all for coming."

CHAPTER 6

Divisible

I LOOKED FORWARD TO spring. One reason was that Dad and I could be outside playing catch with a baseball. Sometimes Liz came out with me and used Dad's glove. We liked living out in the country even though it was a little isolated from other people. We were less isolated because of television was beginning to be our main source of what was going on in the world.

The spring of 1959 was eventful. President Eisenhower signed a bill admitting Alaska to the Union as the 49th State. Hawaii would follow as the 50th in August. That meant we were going to have a new flag with fifty stars. In a design contest, President Eisenhower received hundreds of submissions for the flag from across the country. A 17-year-old, Robert Heft, created a flag as a high school project and got a "B minus" for it. His teacher joked that if it was accepted by Congress as the winner, he would reconsider the grade. Heft's flag won, and he got the "A" he deserved.

We watched a television news story about Fidel Castro, who overthrew dictator Batista in Cuba and then came to visit the United States. He met with Vice President Nixon, because President Eisenhower refused to meet him. Castro later turned out to be a communist, allied with the Soviet Union. While the Cold War with the Soviet Union was often in the news, Dad wanted us to read about the Civil War. He had opened Albert Klund's family Bible and found something he wanted to share with us. I remember how anxious he was to begin after dinner.

That is when Dad asked, "Do you remember the one mystery that we have been trying to solve for almost a year?" He waited for just a few seconds. Then he answered his own question, "We have all these letters and notes, some from more than two hundred years ago, but we don't know who collected and preserved them. Well, we didn't know until now. Look at this family Bible. It reveals some secrets." He turned the Bible and let us see a page that was opened. It was a genealogy of the Klund family.

Dad said, "This is Albert Klund's Bible. His is the third from the last name on the page. He was born in 1824 in Pittsburgh. Albert is my great grandfather. Now look above his name, his father was Harold, and his grandfather was Jacob Klund. Jacob's grandfather was Johan Andrew who wrote the letters from Valley Forge during the American Revolution. Jacob's son, Fredrick, was the one who brought the food and blankets to the camp. I would guess that Johan or his wife Sara began collecting the family letters and records during the Revolution. Or maybe, Frederick, who would have known how his grandfather and grandmother came to America. I checked the style of the trunk. It had to be built around the time of the Civil War. It was Albert's great aunt Joanne's, and she gave it to him. Now we know it was in Grandpa Klund's attic and but we don't know why Grandma didn't tell us about it."

I really appreciate what Albert preserved for us, especially Albert's Bible. This is the *Family Records* page that my dad showed us. It fills in some genealogy that we didn't know.

Johan Jacob Klund b. 1710m. Barbara Holl b. 1714

Johan Andrew Klund b. 1731 m. Sara Schmidt b. 1733

Frederick Klundb. 1753m. Maria O'Toole b. 1752

Jacob Klundb. 1773m. Madeline Drummond b. 1776

Harold Herman K. b. 1796m. Catherine Berkholed b. 1790

Albert Klundb. 1824 m. Clara White b. 1827

John Ross Klund b 1845m. Anna Petit b. 1849

Matthew Klund b. 1868

When we began reading that page, Mom told us the "m" meant married. She also noted that the Bible was very thick and she asked Dad whether there were some loose papers inserted in it. She thought there might be some clues to what we hadn't yet discovered inside those pages.

Dad answered, "Yes, there were three letters and a paper folded inside the pages. We will begin looking at a couple of those today. They are from the Civil War period. Before we read the letters, you should remember how the Civil War started. South Carolina was the first state to leave the Union. Just off the coast of Charleston is Fort Sumter. It was a federal fort, so it belonged to the United States. If South Carolina claimed its independence, it would have to prove its sovereignty by taking over the fort. The Union officer, Robert Anderson, refused to surrender it."

"On April 12th, 1861 Confederate shore batteries in Charleston began to lob shells at the fort. After a day and a half of heavy fire, Anderson raised a white flag. The Civil War had begun. President Lincoln called for 75,000 volunteers to join the Union Army."

"One of those volunteers was Albert Klund. He enlisted at Pittsburgh in 1862 and became a soldier in the 7th Pennsylvania Regiment. Inside the Bible was his first letter home. Will you read it, Mom?" She read:

May 3, 1862

Dear Clara,

Tell the children I am well. I hope John Ross has been willing and able to look after you all. At least he is earning enough to support the family. All the marching has made my feet sore, but it is bearable. We marched through the state, camping and training on the way to Chambersburg. I was accompanying a large wagon train of supplies. When we arrived, word was out that we were going to meet the rebels in the Shenandoah Valley. After a few days, we struck tents and began another long march. We had a regular drill at camp Williams for about a week.

Then we moved toward Williamsport. The first evening there, an alarm sounded and we were called to arms. I heard shots, but no battle commenced. Just a brief skirmish. We are nearing the Potomac, and we know that the rebels are on the other side. I expect we will try to cross in a day or two. General Patterson has the respect of all. The men are encouraged and expecting to seize and hold the entire Shenandoah Valley. As always, pray for us.

Albert

July 4, 1862

Dear Clara,

Today we heard that General McClellan in West Virginia had reached our army of the Shenandoah. Because it was the anniversary of Independence, they fired a national salute. I am proud to serve in the Union Army, but I miss being with you and the children on the holiday.

A few of our soldiers tried to cross the Potomac on the 25th of June. They lost some men and a few horses to gunfire. So, we waited for more soldiers and artillery before trying again. Two days later we began to ford the river. It was an awesome sight; many men were shouting at the top of their lungs. We crossed and marched to Martinsburg. There we found a large supply of grain and flour, and we confiscated it because we heard that the owner was a captain in the Confederate army. We were told not to loot any citizens' homes. I have heard that some of Sheridan's men were not so restrained. We may be marching back into Pennsylvania soon. I am tired but in good spirits. If the president is right, this war will be over soon.

Albert

Dad reminded us that the president was too optimistic; the war would drag on for three more years. Liz said she had studied the Civil War in her history class, so she remembered part of this.

Dad told her that any time she wanted to break in and share something she had learned, she should do it. We agreed to return to the Civil War the following day.

The next evening Dad told us that President Lincoln's main problem was that he could not find a general capable of facing off against the South's Robert E. Lee. But the longer the war lasted, the greater the chance that the North would win. It had more soldiers, more industry, and stronger finances.

Liz interrupted. "I learned that in school; and your forgot that the North had more people and a navy."

Dad smiled, "That is a very good observation, Liz." That may be the reason that Lincoln thought it would not be a long war. Actually, it could have ended sooner."

"Robert E. Lee, the South's best general, knew that a long war favored the North, so he decided to convince the Union Congress to call off the war. He stopped fighting a defensive war and prepared to invade Pennsylvania, maybe even threaten Philadelphia. Lee's Army of Northern Virginia was in great spirits as they moved through the Shenandoah Valley. By July 1st, 1863 they were all the way to Gettysburg, Pennsylvania. There they met General George Mead's Army of the Potomac."

"Mead's men were dug in on the high ground, forcing the Confederate troops to charge across a field and up the heavily armed hill. They made valiant attempts but lost so many men that Lee had to withdraw. Some people believe that if Meade had followed up the victory and chased Lee's troops the war would have ended in 1863. But Meade let Lee get away"

"As you know, President Lincoln was asked to dedicate the National Cemetery at Gettysburg. In his address, he said 'the world will little note nor long remember what we say here.' That was the only thing in the address that was wrong. We have a copy. Who will read it?"

Liz said, "I had to memorize this in history class this year. I will try to quote it." She began,

Four score and seven years ago our fathers brought forth on this continent a new nation, conceived in Liberty, and dedicated to the proposition that all men are created equal.

Now we are engaged in a great civil war, testing whether that nation or any nation so conceived and so dedicated, can long endure. We are met on a great battle-field of that war. We have come to dedicate a portion of that field, as a final resting place for those who here gave their lives that that nation might live. It is altogether fitting and proper that we should do this.

But, in a larger sense, we cannot dedicate—we cannot consecrate—we cannot hallow—this ground. The brave men, living and dead, who struggled here, have consecrated it, far above our poor power to add or detract.

The world will little note, nor long remember what we say here, but it can never forget what they did here. It is for us the living, rather, to be dedicated here to the unfinished work which they who fought here have thus far so nobly advanced. It is rather for us to be here dedicated to the great task remaining before us—that from these honored dead we take increased devotion to that cause for which they gave the last full measure of devotion—that we here highly resolve that these dead shall not have died in vain—that this nation, under God, shall have a new birth of freedom—and that government of the people, by the people, for the people, shall not perish from the earth.

Dad was very impressed. He told Liz that she had recited it perfectly. Maybe she should run for president! That was a good place to end the evening's discussion. Dad told us we could take a break for a few days and then finish the other papers in Albert's Bible.

We didn't go to movies often, but Dad read in the newspaper that *Ben-Hur* was showing in Bethel Park. He said we could go on Friday night. Liz and I were really excited, even though we didn't know who Ben-Hur was.

Wow! What a show! We were spellbound by the grand scenes and captivated by Judah, the Jewish merchant turned slave, his sincere heart and inner strength. It was a great love story that took place in the Roman Empire at the time of Jesus. The scenery was breathtaking. The chariot race took our breath away, and the crucifixion scene was so realistic. We loved the ending when Judah realized all the hatred in his heart had melted away. Charlton Heston became my movie hero.

On Monday, we returned to talking about the Civil War. Dad had another letter and a paper that were folded inside pages of Albert's Bible. Before we read them, he told us that Lincoln finally found his general in Ulysses Grant. He earned his reputation as a fighter in the West, capturing Vicksburg on the Mississippi River. President Lincoln promoted him to lead the final effort to defeat General Lee in Virginia. The letter was from John Ross Klund, Albert's son. He was probably just 19 years old when he wrote from the war zone. Dad read the letter.

> *March 20, 1865*
>
> *Dear Mom,*
>
> *I hope that dad was able to get home safely. He served long enough. Tell him that I am in good health. We have fought long and hard, but Lee's army remains out of our reach. I hear General Grant is weary with all of this. Who knows how many men have died in this blood-soaked land of northern Virginia. Today we blew up a railroad to keep their army from getting the supplies they need. The explosions are still ringing in my ears. We all pray that General Lee soon realizes what a mistake and how costly it would be to prolong this struggle. They cannot win, if we continue pressing forward.*
>
> *I am tired of marching every day and the food is awful, but, thank God we have not lost many men. By the time this letter reaches you I hope the war will be over.*
>
> *John Ross*

Dad told us that the war would soon end and that the nation would be forever changed in a series of rapid events. Civil War cost the nation dearly. First, more than 620,000 people died. The Union spent more than $6 billion, and the Confederacy spent more than $2 billion for its military. The loss of crops and decline in production cost the South billions more. Even worse, freed African Americans and poor whites faced extreme hardship in the South both during and after Reconstruction.

Dad had a paper in his hand. He said, "Here is how President Lincoln assessed the meaning of the war that was still being fought in his second inaugural address to a muddy soaked crowd in Washington D.C.

March 4, 1865

If we shall suppose that American Slavery is one of those offences which, in the providence of God, must needs come, but which, having continued through His appointed time, He now wills to remove, and that He gives to both North and South, this terrible war, as the woe due to those by whom the offence came, shall we discern therein any departure from those divine attributes which the believers in a Living God always ascribe to Him? Fondly do we hope—fervently do we pray—that this mighty scourge of war may speedily pass away. Yet, if God wills that it continue, until all the wealth piled by the bond-man's two hundred and fifty years of unrequited toil shall be sunk, and until every drop of blood drawn with the lash, shall be paid by another drawn with the sword, as was, said three thousand years ago, so still it must be said "the judgments of the Lord, are true and righteous altogether"

With malice toward none; with charity for all; with firmness in the right, as God gives us to see the right, let us strive on to finish the work we are in; to bind up the nation's wounds; to care for him who shall have borne the battle, and for his widow, and his orphan—to do all which may achieve and cherish a just and lasting peace, among ourselves, and with all nations.

Dad said that on the cloudy day when Lincoln finished that address there was a resounding roar of applause. Then, just at that moment, the sun burst through the clouds and flooded the scene with a power and light that astounded everyone. Lincoln told

Journalist Noah Brooks that it made his heart jump. This speech is considered the most powerful one ever delivered in American history. It reveals Lincoln's strong faith in God and his belief that the war was a strong penalty for years of slavery. The conclusion shows that Lincoln meant to be a gracious healer of the nation's wounds when the war ended.

General Lee surrendered to Grant at Appomattox five weeks after the inauguration. Lincoln had been preparing for the aftermath of the war. He faced significant legal decisions. Would the Confederacy be treated as a foreign conquered nation? Would southern leaders be charged or punished for the crime of secession? What would happen to the enslaved people? How would they survive now that they were free?

Dad noticed that we were looking a little disinterested, so he told us we would continue with the end of the Civil War tomorrow. That was ok with me, because it wasn't dark yet, and I wanted to take advantage of the beautiful evening for a bike ride.

The next day, soon after we finished dinner, Dad wanted to wrap up our discussion on the Civil War. He began, "Lincoln's plan for reconstruction of the South gave full pardon and restoration of property to all who engaged in the rebellion except the Confederate officeholders and military leaders. It allowed new state governments to be formed after 10 percent of the eligible voters took an oath of allegiance to the United States. Do you think that was fair?"

We agreed that it probably was fair. Mom said that the South had lost so much already. Some large cities were badly burned and plantation owners lost all their investment in slaves. Railroads had been torn up and many people were homeless.

Dad said, "Mom's right. So, Congress created the Freedmen's Bureau to assist former slaves in the South. General Sherman set up his headquarters at the McLeod plantation outside Charleston, South Carolina. He had a plan to allow former slaves to apply for 40 acres of land all along east coast of the southern states. Much of that land had belonged to wealthy plantation owners."

"President Lincoln was invited to Fort Sumter to raise the American flag where the war started. He turned it down because he was going to the theater to see a play, *My American Cousin*. John Wilkes Booth and his conspirators planned to kill both the president and Secretary of State Seward. Former Civil War soldier, Lewis Powell forced his way into Seward's home and slashed him with a Bowie knife. Seward survived because his head was heavily bandaged after a carriage accident. Booth, an actor, walked into Ford's Theater and fatally shot the president."

"The assassination of Lincoln on April 14, 1865 changed everything. Andrew Johnson, the vice president, was a Democrat from Tennessee. He had been chosen as a running mate during the 1864 election because the Republican party feared Lincoln would lose his reelection bid if he didn't have support in the border states. Johnson killed the plan to distribute land to the former slaves. Then the president and Congress fought each other over how to deal with former Confederates until finally Congress impeached Johnson. He survived removal from office by only one vote."

Mom had heard enough history. She smiled and moved that the meeting be adjourned. Dad laughed out loud. Liz and I slipped out of our chairs grinning at each other.

CHAPTER 7

A Visit to the Past

LIKE THE CIVIL WAR, the school term finally came to an end. It was the time of year when I used to look forward to spending a week at Grandma's house. Liz had her own week there too. Now that we were living in the house, the usual anticipation was gone.

We decided to read the Gospel of Matthew after dinner. Dad said it began with a genealogy—the ancestors of Jesus. After we read and talked about the first half of chapter one, Dad asked us if anyone had something to share. Liz did. She said it was too bad that people had to die. Summer wasn't the same without a trip to Grandma's house. It wasn't the house that made it fun. It was Grandma. We didn't try to cheer her up because we all felt the same way.

The next evening Mom told us we were going to a restaurant to celebrate finishing another school year. We rarely went out to eat, so this was a welcome surprise. We drove to Pittsburgh because Mom remembered that one of the neighbors told her that we would love Sodini's in Squirrel Hill.

Sodini's food was delicious. I was about half-way through my bacon burger when Dad told us there was something he and Mom had been thinking about. Mom took over from there. "We have been talking about how much you missed having a vacation at Grandma's. It is sad that she is not here, and I know the house is not the same. So, we want to do something special this summer. How about taking a road trip to visit some of the places we read about in the old letters?"

"Like Rotterdam?" Liz asked. She said it with a grin because she probably knew we weren't going to Europe.

"No, but how about Eastern Pennsylvania, Maryland, and Virginia," Mom answered. She told us we could spend a few days on the road, stopping at Valley Forge, visiting historic places in Philadelphia and Baltimore, ending at George Washington's home in Mount Vernon. "What do you two think?" We didn't have to think long. All we wanted to know was how soon we could pack our bags.

We did pack our luggage that night because Dad wanted to get an early start in the morning. We got up at seven, ate a quick breakfast, loaded the car, and set off for Philadelphia. Mom brought some sandwiches and Cokes in a picnic basket, because Dad didn't want to stop for lunch.

As we backed out the drive, Mom handed me and Liz a map of Pennsylvania. She had highlighted our route in green. I guess she thought we would be entertained by following our progress on the map. We weren't. Liz and I spent the time looking at billboards and playing the alphabet game. Mom announced each town as we approached. "We are almost to Greensburg, we are close to Bedford, we are in the Cumberland Valley." What we wanted to hear was, "We can eat now." Finally, we stopped at a little park near Gettysburg and had lunch.

Dad told us a little about the Civil War battle when the South invaded Pennsylvania. "We don't have time to stop here today, but maybe on another trip we can take the Gettysburg battlefield tour." Liz looked a little disappointed, then she started to recite the Gettysburg Address. So, we parked and walked over the battlefield. Dad pointed out Little Round Top and Cemetery Ridge. We climbed up and looked down upon the open field where so many Confederates lost their lives. We could almost see them falling and hear the rifle fire.

Soon we were back on the road to Valley Forge where two of our ancestors spent a terrible winter. We arrived in mid-afternoon and went into the Valley Forge Visitor Center to get tickets for a guided tour. While we waited, Dad told us we could each pick out a souvenir. I found a little canon, and Liz chose a replica of an 1860 U.S. flag. The guide was interesting. We walked along the area where the troops came into camp. Then he took us into one of the Muhlenberg huts that the soldiers built. There was very little light inside. It didn't look like a place where I would want to live.

More interesting to me was visiting George Washington's headquarters, a large brick house. We found out that Martha Washington came here to be with her husband. I couldn't help but notice the vast difference between the comforts of the brick headquarters building and the soldiers' little huts with dirt floors. I tried to imagine Andrew sleeping there in front of a fireplace, breathing the smoke and trying to keep warm. The valley was beautiful now, a lot different than when it was home to thousands of suffering soldiers, dead horses, and smoky huts.

We drove toward Philadelphia, ate at a little locally owned restaurant, and checked into a Holiday Inn. We were ready for bed earlier than usual. The next day we saw the Liberty Bell, Independence Hall, and Ben Franklin's house. "This is where the nation was born," the guide at Independence Hall reminded us. I was glad that I knew about the Declaration of Independence and the brave men who signed their names to it right where we were standing. You could feel the history in that room. The guide at Franklin's house said Ben was indeed a genius. We saw the evidence that he was a scientist, an inventor, a printer, a diplomat, and a political philosopher, among other things. This was turning out to be a great vacation.

On the way back to our car, Dad informed us we were going to Lancaster County, where the Klund's first settled in America. Liz and I could hardly wait for that. Soon we were back on the road watching the cows and billboards. About thirty minutes outside Philadelphia we began to see Amish horse buggies. Dad explained that these people tried to live as their ancestors did, a simple life without modern technology, like television and motor vehicles. Mom said they don't want to be photographed; many avoid conversations with outsiders.

"Were the Klunds Amish?" Liz asked. Dad thought that our ancestors were probably Lutheran, because that was the dominant religion of the Palatine in Germany. Mom told us that we were going to stay at a tourist home here in Lancaster County. She said, "The Mennonite family that owns it, also lives a plain lifestyle, but they have electricity, telephones, and cars. And they do not keep separate from other people."

We arrived at a farm with a large barn and beautiful white house with a rambling front porch and several rocking chairs. The lady who opened the door was neatly dressed and wearing an apron over her blue skirt. She said they were expecting us and if we liked we could go upstairs and see our rooms. Dinner would be served at six o'clock in the dining room off to the right of the entrance.

We unloaded our luggage and climbed the stairs. The bedrooms were much nicer than ours at home. "What are we going to do until dinner?" Liz said. Dad thought we could just walk around the farm. But when we got back downstairs, a man introduced himself as Samuel Dirksen and asked us whether we might like to ride some horses. That sounded like great fun. Mom agreed, and she went upstairs to change clothes.

Mr. Dirksen was the owner of the farm. His son, Bryce, got us saddled up, explained how to guide the horses, and assured us that they already knew where to go and what to do. He rode the lead horse, and as we followed around the very large farm, he explained how his family managed it. The ride was fantastic, just a little bumpy. Bryce said we would get used to that. When we came back to the house, dinner was ready. I will never forget that day, the good food, the Dirksens, the quiet evening rocking on the front porch and watching the birds, and the butterflies on the flowers.

We got up early and ate eggs and pancakes almost as good as Mom's. Then we said goodbye and drove south to Baltimore. There we stopped to visit Fort McHenry, where Francis Scott Key wrote the words to the *Star Spangled Banner*. I imagined the bombs bursting in air above the Chesapeake Bay and the huge flag that withstood the explosions of that night.

Liz remembered the Baltimore newspaper we found in the trunk—the one that had the poem that became our national anthem. "Why do you think someone preserved that paper?" she asked.

Mom thought that the person who read it believed it would be historic. Dad thought that it may have been among some other newspapers in a family member's house, but someone later decided to preserve this one because of Francis Scott Key's poem. Either way, we were so glad someone saved it.

We were soon back in the car and on our way to Mount Vernon. I tried to imagine what it would look like and remembered a picture of it I had seen in a book. We stopped for a quick snack and reached Mount Vernon sooner than I thought. It was a beautiful setting, right beside the Potomac river. The guide who took us through the house knew so much. He told us that what looked like stone on the house was just wood siding painted and sprayed with sand to make it look more expensive. Washington inherited the house from his father and he enlarged it to become a mansion. It is 11,000 square feet, with about five or six times as many rooms as our house.

We didn't realize that George Washington was an inventor. He rotated crops and amended the soil. He built a new way for his horses to thresh grain on the floor of a special barn. His management and improvements to the farm helped to make him one of the wealthiest men in America. After serving as president, he came back here, where he died from a throat infection. He and his wife Martha are buried not far from the house.

By late afternoon Dad was ready to be back on the road, going south to Williamsburg and Jamestown. Williamsburg was the capital of colonial Virginia. We visited the House of Burgesses, where Patrick Henry gave his famous "Give me liberty or give me death" speech. I imagined him standing there in front of the delegates waving his arms and putting on a dramatic show. Many of the guides and workers were dressed in colonial costumes, making it seem like we stepped back into history.

We stayed overnight at a hotel on the road to Jamestown. The next day we took a self-guided tour of historic Yorktown. They had set up tents like the ones George Washington's army used, and we saw a movie about the battle. Dad reminded us that this is where the American independence was won.

By noon we were back on the road. We drove home with a better sense of what it took to create the United States, although we didn't talk about that very much. Mom and Dad talked about their work. Liz and I were tired, but she whispered to me "Did you see the beautiful dog that the Dirksen's had?"

I knew immediately what she was thinking. I waited for a pause in Mom and Dad's conversation. Then I said, "Wasn't that a beautiful dog at the Dirksen's? I thought about how much fun we would have if we had a dog like that."

Dad didn't take long to answer. "Yes, it was a fine-looking dog. And you two have been quiet about the dog issue for about two months. So, let's see if we can find a puppy for you when we get back home. I haven't forgotten about the dog or your promises to take care of it."

That was the good news we wanted to hear, and I fell asleep thinking about it. When we got home, it was dark, and I was still asleep in the back seat. I didn't like having to wake up, carry my stuff upstairs, and get ready for bed. I think I was too tired to dream about defending Ft. McHenry or living with George and Martha at Mt. Vernon, or having a new puppy.

The next day, Dad asked us if we would like to help him work on the upstairs guest bedroom. By the look on his face, we knew better than to say "no." So, he told us to put on some old clothes and join him as soon as we were ready. Mom was about to leave on a grocery shopping trip but she wasn't quite out the door when I asked her what I should wear. She suggested my ragged blue jeans and a faded shirt.

Helping Dad turned out to be more fun than we thought. He was finishing patching up the plaster on the wall when he asked us to help clean the floor. "Before we put down the new carpet, I want to paint the room," he said. "I have a can of light blue paint down in the garage. Jacob, it's under the work bench. Could you get it? And Liz, I need a couple of old rags and a bucket of warm water. The bucket and rags are in the garage." We went on our errands and were back in a few minutes.

"Ok, kids, check the walls and wipe off any dirt or bits of wet plaster or anything that would show through the paint. Then wipe up anything that's on the floor. I am going to stir the paint and give you each a brush. Wait a minute, we need to use the masking tape." We worked to get the walls and floor ready and taped off the windows and baseboard. Then we went downstairs for lunch. Mom had lunch ready, and we took our time eating the sandwiches and potato salad while the plaster upstairs dried.

By mid-afternoon we were ready to paint. While Dad used a roller, we took our brushes and painted all the edges. When Dad finished off the top border, the room looked brand new. Then we went back downstairs to help Dad bring up the carpet. We helped him roll it out. He said, "Jacob, can you pick up that night stand and put it in the hall?" We had worked around that little piece of furniture. Dad said it was the only thing left in the room after the estate sale that they held at Grandma's house. I lifted it, but it felt heavier than it looked. I opened the one top drawer. There were four stacks of cards, each tied together with a string. On top of each stack was a picture of a baseball player. The uniforms looked very different from what the ball players I knew wore. I said, "Hey Dad, look at this."

Dad came over and looked in the drawer. "Oh my goodness!" Oh, my goodness!"

I said, "What's the matter?"

"Nothing at all, Jacob. I just can't believe that these cards are here. They were mine when I was a kid. I thought I had lost them. I left them in my room when I went off to college. I did not recognize this night stand, because someone has painted it. You have no idea how great this is." He picked up a bundle of cards and untied the string. A guy named Hank Greenburg was on top.

Dad said, "Some of these are probably in good enough condition to sell to collectors. But I think I will just keep them. Here look." Dad leafed through the stack. "I remember a few names, like Dizzy Dean, Lefty Gomez, Luke Appling, and of course, Babe Ruth. Every kid knows that one." As I was looking at the cards, Dad disappeared. I asked Liz where he was. She told me he went downstairs, probably to tell Mom about our find.

Dad came back up and told us he just had to tell Mom. He said, "Jacob, I think you have the finders touch, first the trunk and now the cards. I think this deserves a trip to Yeagers Ice Cream tonight." He told me to go ahead and move the stand to the hall. He took the cards over to his bedroom, and we helped him roll out the carpet and held it down while he pulled it to the edges. After he tacked down the threshold, we stood back and surveyed the room. Liz said, "A threshold is good to hold down the carpet, but why is it called "threshold?"

Dad said "Great question. Way back before colonial times, most poor people didn't have carpets. Their floors were dirt, and they kept floors from turning into a muddy mess by using straw from threshing wheat to cover the floor. Wind and foot traffic in and out could move the thresh out the door. So, they put a wood plank across the opening to hold in the thresh—a threshold."

Liz asked Dad if there was any history he didn't know. He laughed and said, "A lot more than you could ever imagine! The room looks great, thanks for helping. Let's bring up the furniture and put up the bed."

We helped carry a dresser, chair, and bed from the garage up to the room. They were some of the nicest pieces that had belonged to Grandma. I learned how a bed is put together. Dad called down to Mom and asked where the bed clothes were. She told us to look on the left side of the hall closet. That's Mom; she always knows where everything is. We made the bed and stood back again to survey our work. Mom brought two pictures to hang on the wall. When we finished, the room looked like a magazine photo.

We took a break and rode out bikes for a while. When we came back Mom was in the kitchen cooking dinner. We could smell it. So, the three of us hurried to wash up. "What smells so good?" Liz asked. Mom revealed a big dish of Chinese chop suey and a bowl of rice. We dug into that and then we all hopped in the car and went to get some Yeager's ice cream.

The next day Dad said he wanted to talk about our vacation trip. "Anything you want to discuss?" There was a moment of silence because we weren't sure what he meant. Mom was the first to respond. She said she had been thinking about how the country began, the courage and beliefs of the men and women who lived then. "Do you think we are the same kind of people today?"

Nobody talked, so I answered. "I don't think I would have had the courage to spend a winter in one of those huts at Valley Forge."

Dad thought that was a really good "admission." Then he explained, "The people who lived in that time were much more used to hardship than we are. They faced so many more serious challenges, and I think it made them tougher. But Americans seem to rise to the occasion in every generation. When we were attacked in World War II, thousands of people committed to put their lives in jeopardy to defend the country. I enlisted, knowing it would be a tough test for me. I guess I was a little too young to realize the seriousness of that decision. But there is one thing that carried over from the Revolution to then; it was the belief in God and the trust that He would be with us."

"On D Day, before the planned invasion in Normandy, President Roosevelt went on the radio and prayed for the nation. I don't have a copy of that prayer, but I think it included a prayer for all the troops and a request that those who lost their lives would be with Him in heaven. And General Eisenhower's final message to the troops at Normandy was, 'And let us all beseech the blessing of Almighty God upon this great and noble undertaking.' Men on board the ships that were to deliver them to the shore bowed their heads as the chaplains prayed."

Mom added, "The Christian influence on America is recorded throughout our history. So, belief in an eternal life is the best foundation for sacrifice of our personal ambitions to that of others, especially for their country."

Dad agreed, and then he changed the subject, "Before we finish, I want to let you know that I found a family in Pleasant Hill that raises dogs. They have some puppies for sale. Do you want to go over and see them this weekend?"

"Yes," Liz and I said together. We were pretty excited as we went out to our bikes. And we were both so proud of Dad, and glad Mom chose to marry a man like him. Looking back on those years, I do feel some nostalgia those days when most of our friends had good parents, when so many people went to church, and when President Eisenhower signed a bill that added "under God," to the pledge of allegiance.

On the surface, our society seemed to be on a solid foundation of faith. But most people didn't realize that foundation was being eroded. The public education system was beginning to show signs of it. I was too young to be aware of that. But our family was about to be awakened.

On Saturday Dad took us to a small farm on the other side of Pleasant Hill. They had two litters of puppies ready for sale. We were allowed to hold them and see which one we liked most. One little Scottie snuggled right up to us. That's all we wanted to know. Dad paid for the puppy and we took turns holding her all the way home.

The next thing we had to do was to name the puppy. We all had ideas, and it seemed we would never agree. Then Mom said, I just hope she grows up to be a fine lady. Liz brightened up and said, "Let's call her Lady." We all thought that was who she should be.

The school term started the first week of September. I was going into sixth grade and Liz was starting eighth. Dad had a new teaching assignment—one that he had wanted for a long time. He would be teaching American history to juniors in the eleventh grade. He was also teaching ninth grade civics.

Just before school started, Mom got a job. That summer she had told us she wanted to find work where she could use her biology degree. One of the neighbors mentioned that Allegheny

County was looking to hire an assistant in the South Park Nature Center. Mom visited the center and was hired within a week. That meant Dad had to find a car for her to get to work. It turned out great, because one of Dad's teacher friends decided to buy a new car, and he sold his to us for $900.

That summer we had spent so much time on our history discussions. With school starting again, we decided to have family sharing time and Bible reading after dinner for the next several weeks.

One evening in October, Dad came home with news. He told us that he had read an educational journal that described two court cases that could possibly affect our schools. The first was in New York. There the state had composed a prayer for students to say at the beginning of each school day. Some people were challenging that as a violation of the First Amendment. Dad said that actually, the First Amendment says, "Congress shall make no law respecting the establishment of religion." But these people thought that a state-composed prayer to be said in schools was unconstitutional.

The other case was right here in Pennsylvania—Abington Township. Some parents were challenging Pennsylvania's law that says schools should read ten verses of the Bible every day. Once again, the First Amendment simply limits Congress, not Pennsylvania, from making a law establishing religion. So, the lower courts upheld both New York and Pennsylvania. But Dad was worried that the Supreme Court likely would not. Mom asked how he could be so sure about that.

Dad explained. "The Supreme Court has changed a lot in the last twenty years. In the 1930s, Franklin Roosevelt replaced eight judges. Most of them were progressives, while the retiring justices were conservative. Conservative meant that they applied the law exactly as the Constitution intended. Progressives used the Constitution to promote their own views of fairness and justice."

Dad continued, "President Eisenhower appointed Chief Justice Earl Warren. I am not sure how his leadership affects the Court, but I fear the progressives are in the majority. Prayer and Bible reading in public schools could be found unconstitutional.

Who knows what the effects of that would be. We will just have to wait and see what the Supreme Court says."

Chapter 8

Other Revolutions

September was unusually rainy, more than any September we could remember. Liz and I liked to be outside in the Fall, but many evenings were too wet to do much. Some of our friends came over to the house to play Monopoly or other board games. After a few weeks, Dad took advantage of the family sharing time to get back into the family history. We were more than half way through the contents of the trunk, and we still didn't know how it got into Grandma Klund's attic, or why she never talked about it.

One evening, after we ate our pizza, Dad told us that he had some wedding photos and other things to share with us. He reached behind his chair to a pile of papers on the buffet. The first thing he showed us was a marriage certificate for John Ross Klund and Anna Petit. They were married in 1867. Then Dad opened up a folder with some wedding pictures. We finally could put faces on people we had only read about. Anna Petit was a beautiful woman. She looked like a person we would like to know. Liz said, "She must have been a good Mom because our Grandma, who she raised, was one of the nicest people we knew."

At the bottom of the stack was a notebook. Dad said it was an old business ledger. On the front was the name, Thomson Steel Works. Dad told us that Andrew Carnegie built it, his first steel company, in 1872. He named the plant after J. Edgar Thompson, the president of the Pennsylvania Railroad. Inside the cover was a stamp, "J.R. Klund Accountant." The title on the first page was Accounts Receivable.

The ledger book listed Carnegie's clients with purchase orders, shipping dates, and receivables. Each page contained the sales of steel to clients like the Pennsylvania Railroad, Beaver Creek Railroad, Baltimore & Ohio, New York Central, Keystone Bridge Co. At the bottom of each page was a signature, sometimes by Andrew Carnegie himself. Dad said that John R. Klund may have been one of Carnegie's accountants.

Then Dad told us a little about Andrew Carnegie. He came with his parents—immigrants from Scotland to the Pittsburgh area at age 13. After working for about a nickel a day in a cotton mill, he learned to send telegraph messages and became the personal telegraph operator for Thomas Scott, the general superintendent of the Pennsylvania Railroad.

Through saving and investing in start-up companies Carnegie built a fortune. He consolidated his companies into Carnegie Steel, the biggest steel producer in the world. His companies were the most efficiently run businesses in the country. A big part of that efficiency was his idea of owning the iron ore mines, railroads, and steel plants. He saved a ton of costs by not having to buy from other suppliers or carriers.

By the age of 35 Carnegie was a multimillionaire. There were many such businessmen in the Industrial Revolution: John D. Rockefeller, whose Standard Oil Company had a near monopoly on the oil business. There was J. P. Morgan, Henry Ford, Leland Stanford and others. Some hoarded their money, but several believed in sharing their success. Andrew Carnegie became a philanthropist. I asked Dad what that was. Dad explained, "It's a person who gives large sums to support worthy causes. Carnegie built libraries all across the country, because he believed a reading public was vital to democracy. He wrote an article called 'Wealth,' later published as 'The Gospel of Wealth,' explaining the strategic ways that wealthy people could help their communities."

"The city of Pittsburgh became the steel center of the Industrial Revolution, and Carnegie was largely responsible for that. You know the name of our professional football team, don't you?"

"Yah, it's the Steelers," I answered. "Now I know why they chose that name. When did they start playing, was it back when Carnegie lived?"

"No, that came later" dad said, "The owner, Art Rooney, had a football team called the Pirates in 1933, but in 1940 he wanted a different name than the baseball team, so he ran a naming contest in the Pittsburgh Post-Gazette. The winning name was Steelers, submitted by a number of people; one of them was Joe Santorini. Do you remember that name?"

"Yes, Liz said, "It was the restaurant we went to just before summer vacation."

"Right," Dad said, "Now let's get back to our family history.

Mom broke in, "No, the restaurant is Sandini's, not Santorini's.

Dad laughed,"Well I guess you got me there. I have so much to learn! Another thing I didn't know is that my grandfather worked for Andrew Carnegie. It must have been when he was young. I knew him when he was a teamster, like a truck driver today, only with horses. Maybe he lost his accounting job in a recession. You know, he died when I was only five."

Liz said, "Kinda like our grandfather, I think I was only six or seven when he died, wasn't I?"

Mom agreed , "Yes, and probably you don't remember him, do you, Jacob?"

I said that I didn't quite, but I think I remembered him when I saw his picture in our family album and on the mantel in Grandma's house. The mantel was one of the things that they never changed when we moved in. It was sad to see that a lot of Grandma's furniture and stuff was gone when we moved our furniture in. It was probably better for us not to keep too much of her things. We needed the space to make the house our home. I was glad that we did keep some of Grandma's furniture in the guest bedroom.

The next evening, after dinner we had family sharing time. Dad told us that he had a nice surprise. He was going to take us to a Pirates baseball game at Forbes Field. There was a young player that he wanted us to see. The Pirates were playing the Milwaukee Braves that week. The guy that Dad was so interested in was Roberto Clemente, from Puerto Rico. He was beginning his fourth year with the Pirates and already having a big impact on the team.

On Wednesday, we didn't have time for any talk after dinner. We wanted to get to the ballgame early to watch the warmups. There was a big crowd at Forbes Field; Milwaukee always had a good team, and the rivalry was intense. They had Hank Aaron who could hit the ball a mile. The game was great; each team fought back to take the lead. Aaron hit a home run, but Roberto Clemente showed us why he was going to be a star. He had two hits and drove in a run. The Pirates managed to win 6 to 5. They were getting better each year.

The very next year, 1960, the Pirates won the World Series. I will never forget the final game. Everybody thought the Yankees were the better team. But the Pirates won three of the first six, forcing a final showdown. The lead went back and forth, but in the last inning Bill Mazeroski, Pittsburgh's gold glove second baseman, hit a home run to win it. The steel city went wild. We weren't there because tickets were impossible to get, but we saw the whole thing on television. That game has been called the greatest in World Series history.

Well, I had better get back to 1959. More surprises were in store for us. Liz had nearly won our district spelling bee when she was in sixth grade. Now she was entering again with high hopes, because a boy from Pennsylvania had won in 1954, and a girl from the Pittsburgh area had won in 1956. Liz was studying hard, sometimes for two hours a day. The first contest was at Dad's high school. We were excited go and to see it.

After many rounds only three students were still in it, and Liz was one. The first boy missed his word, "synonymous." Liz got it right. Then it went back and forth between Liz and another guy until he missed the word "fracas." Liz spelled the word correctly and won the spelling bee. Dad was extremely proud because he had explained what the word "fracas" meant when we were studying the French and Indian War.

All Western Pennsylvania participating schools sent their champions to Pittsburgh a week or so later. Liz was nervous about this, but Mom was able to get her calmed down before we arrived at the city. The contest was held in Squirrel Hill at a university assembly hall. Liz was really performing well. Again, she survived until there were only three students left. We were on the edge of our seats. Then Liz missed "chihuahua." The next girl got it right. Liz was disappointed, but we gave her some encouragement. Dad said he was so impressed with how calm she was. Mom said, "You probably would have spelled that last word right if we had a tiny dog."

Dad laughed and said, "Let's find some good ice cream on the way home." Nobody objected to that. We found an Islay's ice cream shop before leaving the city. That was a winning choice for all of us.

We had family sharing time for the next few days, because Mom wanted to talk with us about school. We read the Beatitudes and discussed what each of those attributes meant. I liked the "Blessed are the merciful, for they shall obtain mercy," and "Blessed are they that mourn, for they shall be comforted." That was how I felt at Grandma's funeral when the minister said, "We will all miss her, and it hurts with a big emptiness inside, but she is where she was destined to be. And we will see her again. Heaven is only a breath away."

We didn't get to talk about school until the following day. Then Mom asked us how it was going. Liz was feeling better about the spelling bee. Her teacher told her she was one of the best spelling students she had ever had. I told Mom I was doing well in most subjects, but I was having some trouble with word problems in math. Dad offered to spend some time with me on Saturdays. He said, "You can do this, Jacob. You just need to learn how to envision the problem in your mind." I wondered where else I could envision the problem if it wasn't in my mind.

The next evening, we had family prayer for Uncle Rudolph who was in the hospital with some kind of infection. Dad seemed a little worried about it. Mom told him the doctors and hospitals in Philadelphia were very good, but God was even better.

On Friday, when Dad came home, he went directly upstairs, without saying anything to us. This was a little unusual. So, we wondered whether something was wrong. The evening meal was TV dinners because Mom was working at the park that day. TV dinners were frozen meals that came in a package that could be heated in the oven. They got that name because they required little preparation time, and families could sit and watch tv while eating them. We were so traditional that we continued to sit around the table for every meal.

After dinner, Dad said he wanted to tell us something he was thinking about. We thought it was about his brother, Rudolph, but it wasn't. He said there was nothing to be worried about, but he had been thinking about the future for all of us. I wondered why.

Dad told us it was a little complicated. "Did you know that this year is the one-hundredth anniversary of Darwin's book, *On the Origin of Species*?" We didn't. "That was a book that introduced the theory that all life has evolved on the earth from simple to more complex organisms. He called it evolution through natural selection. The fittest animals survived, the others died. Over a long period of time new life forms evolved. In short, monkeys or apes are our humans' ancestors. This book had an immediate impact in Europe and was accepted by some scientists in America. In this century, European Darwinism spread through the American academic community. University science educators generally adopted it first."

"Up to now, the theory of evolution has not had a large effect on public schools. In fact, in the 1920s, Tennessee banned the teaching of evolution. Then there was a trial, often called the Scopes Monkey Trial, because a substitute teacher, John Scopes, said he was teaching Darwin's theory in Dayton Tennessee schools. Actually, the American Civil Liberties Union set up the case, so that it could challenge the state's law. The State of Tennessee won, but the universities and some publishers made evolution a standard part of biology."

Dad explained his concern, "Congress recently passed the National Defense Education Act, because many legislators fear the United States is falling behind the Soviet Union. That act supports textbooks produced with input from the American Institute of Biological Sciences, an organization that believes evolution is the unifying principle of all biology. With evolution through natural selection as the creator of life, there is no need for God."

"That's not the only problem; Christianity also faces a serious challenge in the courts. Right now, we are following the two court cases that have been sent to the United States Supreme Court. Both deal with religion in pubic schools. One challenges Bible reading, the other prayer. In New York, students recite a standard prayer every day. Here we read a few verses from the Bible. Both states' courts have upheld these laws. But I am not optimistic about what will happen in the United States Supreme Court."

Mom asked, "How could you guess what the Supreme Court is going to rule?"

Dad explained, "The Court has changed a lot since we were students. Franklin Roosevelt was president for a long time. He replaced several justices. Most of them are liberal and likely would support the same ideology as their university law schools. That means freedom *from* religion in the public schools. In 1948 the Court ruled that religious instruction in public schools was a violation of the establishment clause in the Constitution."

Mom said, "So, what difference do you think it would make if you just stopped reading a few scriptures to the kids each morning?"

Dad thought a moment. Then he answered, "I have had the same thought. It's likely that many students wouldn't care. Probably, there would be no immediate effect. But let's think in the longer term. Our society has been strongly religious, mostly Christian, for three hundred years. Christianity has been a stabilizing factor. Franklin Roosevelt even prayed for the nation on the radio in World War II."

"I don't know what kind of society we will have if we let our foundational beliefs crumble. If God is removed from all public places, what will happen? We have a few rather chilling histories of that. France tried to do it in the 1790s. Their revolution resulted in mass chaos, wars, and terrible violence. The NAZIS allowed scientists to experiment on humans, like they were animals in Germany. The Soviet communists killed untold numbers of believers and are still persecuting the church. China has a tyrannical dictatorship that massacres millions of people."

"It's the long term here in America and the lives of Liz and Jacob's children that I worry about. Remember, in times of crisis, it was the mostly the Christian community that pledged their lives, their fortunes, and their *sacred* honor to defend freedom." He emphasized the word sacred.

Mom said she understood what he was saying. But she asked Dad what he could do about it. "You are only one teacher," she said. Dad said he was thinking hard about that very issue. Then he said, "We should do what we usually do when we have decisions to make. Pray." That's what we did.

CHAPTER 9

World Leadership

THANKSGIVING WAS APPROACHING, AND I looked forward to a few days off from school. I was doing a little better at math, but a break from that was welcome. Liz had found a really good friend at school in Becky Sabo. She lived a few miles away from us, but sometimes on Saturday her mom or dad would drive her over to our house and let her stay for most of the day. I didn't eavesdrop on their conversation in the bedroom, but I could hear the laughs and giggles as I passed by the hall.

One evening we were watching television after dinner. Dad wanted to see a news special on Dr. Martin Luther King, Jr. He was the pastor of Dexter Avenue Baptist church in Montgomery, Alabama. The announcer said he was in the spotlight as a civil rights leader. He also said King had resigned as pastor of his church and was moving to Atlanta in order to work with the SCLC.

I waited until the program was over to ask Dad some questions, like what was the SCLC? He told me Dr. King started the Southern Christian Leadership Conference to promote civil rights. Blacks were segregated and discriminated against in many states. Segregated means separated, like having separate rest rooms, busses, and schools for blacks.

Dad said, "One example was what happened in Little Rock, Arkansas. The Supreme Court in a case called *Brown* vs. *the Board of Education of Topeka, Kansas* had ruled that segregation in public schools was unconstitutional. When Central High School in Little Rock, Arkansas refused to admit a handful of black students, President Eisenhower ordered the National Guard to Little Rock. Governor Orville Faubus had to back down."

"Dr. King wants to increase the speed of integration and end discrimination against blacks. Integration is giving blacks the same opportunities in school and other environments as whites have. It's the opposite of segregation, or keeping them separate. Discrimination means being treated as lesser; like giving whites preference in hiring. King is an excellent speaker for his cause and may be the most recognized leader of the civil rights movement. We may see more of him in the nightly news."

Two Sundays before Thanksgiving our pastor asked for those who were interested in helping to provide a dinner for some poor families in our county to meet after church in the basement. Mom and Dad went and volunteered to bring a turkey to the church on Tuesday before Thanksgiving. Families were invited to come and pack Thanksgiving boxes.

Liz and I stayed home with Lady. She was growing into a pretty little dog. Mom brought a book about dog training from the library, and we began to teach her some simple commands. She was smart, but a little stubborn. Dad said the Scotties tended to be that way, but they love to play. So, we bought her some chewable toys and doggie treats. She loved to run in the yard, and she was already going outside to "do her business."

On Monday after dinner we got back into the contents of the trunk. Dad said that there were only a few more letters and notes left to read. But he brought an old Colliers magazine from the trunk and opened it to a page that he had marked. He began to read the article.

The Shooting of President McKinley

For the third time a pistol shot has added a sad chapter to American history and created consternation throughout the world. President McKinley was shot down by an assassin while he stood in the Temple of Music at the Buffalo

Exposition on Friday afternoon, September 6, greeting his
fellow citizens.

He stood amiably greeting the people, shaking hands and
exchanging a few words with them until about four o'clock
in the afternoon. At that hour a man in the line whose
hand was seemingly bandaged presented himself to Mr.
McKinley. As he took the president's hand with his own
left, he produced a revolver covered with the false bandage
in his right hand.

Dad said, "He shot the president twice. I won't read the rest to you. You can do that if you like later. An anarchist is a person who would rather have no government at all. This anarchist's name was Leon Czolgosz. The Marine Guard wrestled him to the ground, and he was executed a few weeks later. McKinley was rushed to a hospital where he lingered for several days and physicians tried to save him, but they could not."

Liz, asked, "So who became the president?"

Dad said, "Good question. The Constitution provides for this. The vice president becomes president. Theodore Roosevelt, the vice president, was in Vermont. He hurried to Buffalo as soon as he heard about the shooting. Eight days later, we had a new president. Big changes were on the way for the American government."

"Roosevelt had gained fame by leading a fighting unit called the Rough Riders in the Spanish American War. Unlike McKinley, he was a progressive reformer, the first of three presidents in what we call the Progressive Era because of all the reforms that the federal and state governments adopted between 1900 and 1917. Presidents Roosevelt, Taft, and Wilson all claimed to be progressives."

Mom said she remembered reading about "Muckrakers," but didn't remember how they fit into progressivism. Dad told us they were journalists who exposed corruption, like raking in the muck. Much of the reform movement was a response to their articles. Magazines, newspapers, and books aroused the reading public with exposés such as the corruption in all levels of government, shady business deals, and poor working and sanitary conditions in factories.

Dad said, "The federal government became much more powerful. The president read Upton Sinclair's book *The Jungle*. It described unsanitary conditions in the meat industry. He told Congress to address the issue, and Congress passed the Meat Inspection Act, giving the federal government authority to inspect plants where meat was processed. Congress also created a Federal Reserve System to control our money. The government amended the Constitution to make Senate elections more democratic, and it made the production and sale of alcohol illegal."

I asked Dad when it became legal again. "That amendment was overturned in 1933. In fact, most of the progressive movement faded away when the United States entered World War I. President Wilson, a Democrat, was elected in 1912. In 1916 his campaign slogan was 'He kept us out of war.' But shortly after his reelection, we declared war on Germany."

Liz asked why we declared war on Germany. The history teacher in Dad appeared. "The reason it was called a world war is that Britain, France, and Russia were fighting Germany, Austria-Hungary, and Turkey. The United States joined the war after German submarines began sinking our merchant ships. They wanted to prevent our trade with Britain. We also feared that American investors would lose the money they had invested in Britain if they lost. The final straw was that the British intercepted a telegram in which Arthur Zimmerman, a German foreign secretary, proposed a military alliance with Mexico and offered to help them regain territories they had lost to the United States in our war with Mexico."

"We sent more than 2 million troops to the battlefields of Europe, and about 116,000 of them died. Total deaths in this disastrous war amounted to more than 9 million. Russia, France, Germany, and Austria-Hungary lost millions of soldiers. One of our ancestors was there and came back alive. His letters home will give us a better understanding of conditions on the battlefront. You might know him; he's your grandfather and my dad, Peter. Now we are getting closer to our present family. Are you ready to hear this?"

We all together said yes. Dad was a little emotional when he read,

July 10, 1917

"Dear Mom and Dad,

We arrived here at St. Naizaire, France about two weeks ago. It was comforting to be led in by a battleship escort. No German subs in sight. Thank God they didn't know where we would land. The French are so welcoming; a large crowd gathered to cheer us. It is raining really hard today as we try to set up camp. Working in the heat is uncomfortable, but at least we are safe here.

Gen. Pershing ordered a period of training before we move into the trenches. We have physical drills and usually a long run before breakfast. Then there are platoon and musketry drills. It will probably take a few weeks until all is ready to go. We need supply lines, communications, and other preparations.

Tell Dorothy that I am ok. Someday, after all this is over we will probably get married. Please keep this to yourself.

Love,

Peter

Dad explained that the American troops were not ready to fight; we had only a small standing army. The British called our guys "Doughboys," because they were so untrained. It would take a few months of training before they were even sent to Europe and more before they were sent to the front. He had another letter from Peter. Mom read it to us.

October 28, 1918

Dear Mom and Dad.

We arrived here in Nancy and joined the Luneville trenches last week. I could never have imagined what this would be like. When it rains we are knee deep in muddy water, and there was very little movement on this front. I

got leg cramps just from crouching down every time I tried to walk.

There was no place to sleep. We were not allowed fires or kerosene. It is miserable, wet, and dark by early evening. We knew to keep our heads down to avoid shelling. I was on sentry duty several nights, and I didn't like the thought of looking out over the trench for those nasty Germans. They are only about fifty yards away from our trench and the flash of their rifles and machine guns is just an instant before the thuds on our sandbags. But their flashes gave us a target to return fire. We lost a couple of good men this week. They weren't careful to keep their heads down. It was too dangerous to try to move their bodies out of the trench, so we just had to walk around them. This is so unthinkable.

Nobody wants this war to end more than I do. But I don't see it happening any time soon. Both sides are dug in and a charge over the top of the trench would be disastrous. I had a little break. Several of us were allowed to sneak out for a few days under cover of night. That's how I was able to write to you. Keep me in your prayers.

Love to all, Peter

Dad told us that Grandpa breathed in mustard gas, a terrible weapon that the Germans were using to disable their enemy. He was no longer able to fight, so the army discharged him to be hospitalized in Philadelphia before the end of the war. He recovered well enough in two months to be sent home.

After a few weeks back in Pittsburgh, Grandpa got a job at Westinghouse as an accountant. Uncle Rudolph and I were born after he started working there. When the economy crashed in the 1930s, he lost that job. I was only 12 and Uncle Rudolph was 10 when your grandpa got part-time work for an auto repair shop and a trucking company. Rudolph and I worked for a farmer on our road. We didn't make any money, because we were paid in eggs, milk, and vegetables.

Grandpa returned to a full-time position with Westinghouse when World War II broke out. He was never really healthy, and not breathing well in the city, so they sold their house and moved to Pleasant Hill. Because of the lingering effects of the mustard gas on his lungs, he died of pneumonia in 1945. Grandma kept the house, and after a few years Uncle Rudolph and I helped her with the monthly payments on the mortgage of this old Victorian house.

I was curious about Gandma Klund, so I asked Dad. "Where did Grandma Klund live before she was married?

Dad said, "We should have talked about this years ago. I'm sorry. Grandma Klund was Dottie Gault before she married Grandpa. She grew up on a farm in Kentucky. When she was only 19 years old, she went with a friend from school to find a job in Pittsburg during World War I. She met your grandpa there and married him just a few months after he got home from the Philadelphia hospital. I was born the next year."

Liz asked Dad about his time in the army in World War II. Dad said, "It's still not easy to talk about that. I had started going to college in 1939, so I had more than two years of courses when we declared war on Japan. I quit school in January, 1942 to join the army. I was discharged just in time to see my Dad in the hospital for a few weeks before he died. I really regretted not being there when my parents needed me most."

Dad was getting choked up. Mom broke in, "There really wasn't much you could do, Al; I think they understood."

Liz broke in, "They were probably proud of you for serving the country in the war."

I had to say something, "We are all proud of you, Dad."

We must have said the right things, because Dad smiled and said, come on over here and give me a big hug.

The next evening, when we had family sharing time, Dad said he wanted to talk about his big decision. At first, we didn't know what he was talking about. Mom asked him if he meant what to do about continuing to teach in public school.

"Yes, that's it." Dad said. "I am still studying this, but I want to keep everyone in the know on what I am finding out. I'm reading about the history of public education in America. Unlike so much of the world, the British colonists believed that everyone should have an education. Part of this was the strong belief that people should be able to read the Bible for themselves."

Dad picked up a copy of his notes and read to us, "Massachusetts passed a law that every town of 50 families had to have a free elementary school. After the Revolution, the government passed the Northwest Ordinance, a plan for building states in the Northwest Territory. That's all the Great Lakes states. The Ordinance provided acreage in each township for public education. Three years later, Pennsylvania passed a law providing for free education for all poor people. The people who could afford tutors were expected to educate their own children. The first public high school opened in Boston in 1820."

Dad looked up from his reading, "So you see, education was always considered a vital part of American life. Boston and many other areas were about to experience a wave of Irish immigrants. Just like they felt about the first Germans in Pennsylvania, the people of Massachusetts feared the Irish would change the culture. Most Irish were Catholic, and they tended to cluster together and control their own schools and to keep their kids out of public schools run by Protestants."

From his notes, Dad read, "Most of the states made elementary education compulsory shortly after the Civil War. Republicans and African Americans rewrote state constitutions in the South to offer free public education to all. When president Hayes ended Reconstruction in 1876, public funding for those schools ended."

"There was a huge influx of Polish and Eastern European immigrants after 1890. Like the Irish, these people didn't want their children in public schools. So, they started Catholic or parish schools. By 1900 there were thousands of them, staffed by Catholic sisters."

"So, what did we learn?" Dad asked. Mom said, "I guess we learned that education has been changing as the country responded to waves of immigration."

Dad agreed, "That's what I wanted you to see. And our public schools will continue to respond to more changes. Many Christians are already unhappy with the move toward teaching evolution exclusively as science. I am not sure, but I suspect that if the Supreme Court decides to remove all reference to God from our schools, there will be some Christians who will be left with little choice but to build their own schools, just as the Catholics did many years ago. Others may take advantage of state programs that allow home schooling."

"So, what should I do? I want to be ready to deal with the changes. At this point, I think I would stay in public school teaching, and I hope other Christian teachers would do the same. Without the stabilizing influence of Christian teachers, it's hard to say what would happen in public schools. But I wouldn't blame Christian parents for wanting to get their children out of a totally secular educational environment. And if a homeschooling movement begins in our state, I think I would offer to help it."

Mom told us that she believed Dad would do the right thing, and we should all keep this decision in our prayers. She said that whatever Dad decided to do she would support his decision. I was proud of Mom. There were times when Dad and Mom disagreed and argued, but they seemed to love and respect each other through it all.

On Sunday afternoon after Thanksgiving, the Steelers beat the Eagles 31–0. Dad and I watched it on television. The game and a pizza made it a great afternoon. Mom took Liz in the car to her office at the park to help her set up some displays to an upcoming open house. I took Lady outside to fetch a rubber ball.

When I came back in, Dad asked me whether I liked the family genealogy and history discussions. I told the truth, that I liked them most of the time, except when the history lesson went too long. Dad said he would try to keep it shorter in the future, but we were almost done with the trunk contents. I was a little sad about that.

The next evening, Dad opened the conversation with a question, "How do you think all that stuff got into the trunk and grandma never said anything to us about it?" We were stumped. Dad said he thought he had the answer to that mystery. Now we were "all ears."

"Ok, Dad said, "Remember that Grandpa fought in World War I and breathed in mustard gas. Well, he was never completely well from then on. But he did leave a note in the old family Bible. I found it this week. Remember, the army put him in a Philadelphia hospital. When he was released, he remembered that he had a great aunt living somewhere near the city. So, he looked her up in a phone book. He called and talked to Aunt Joanne, and she invited him to her house. He took a bus to Chester and walked up to an old stone house."

"Your Grandpa and Aunt Joanne had a happy reunion. She told him how she missed James, her husband. And then she told Grandpa that James had a trunk of old letters and stuff, and would he like to see it? She took him upstairs to an unused bedroom. There was the trunk at the foot of the bed, and when your Grandpa looked through it he knew it should be preserved. Aunt Joanne told him he could have it. So, he had it shipped to this house."

"My Dad was not well, but he had to work, so I think he just kept putting off sorting out the trunk contents. Grandma probably knew it was in the attic, but she was not a person to pry. So, she probably just forgot about it. Of all the great things and sacrifices my dad made for us, the trunk is among the most wonderful."

When Dad stopped talking, none of us knew what to say. Finally, Mom just stood up, said "mystery solved," and put her arms around him. Liz said, "Don't they look cute?" That changed the solemn atmosphere, and we all laughed out loud.

CHAPTER 10

The Greatest Generation

CHRISTMAS COULDN'T COME SOON enough. After we finished reading through the trunk collection, we were back to family sharing time after dinner. We read the Christmas story from the gospels. Each time, we found something that we hadn't seen before. This year we read about Jesus' dedication at the temple.

Simeon was the priest on duty that day. Dad said that the Jews kept precise records of who served at the temple every day. The priests rotated, taking turns. Dad thought Jesus might have been dedicated on a Sunday because Genesis says God spoke "Let there be light," on the first day of the week. And Jesus claimed, "I am the light of the world." God told Simeon that he would not die until he had seen the Messiah. When he took Jesus into his arms he said, "Now let your servant die in piece, as you have promised, I have seen your salvation which you have prepared for all people."

Dad said, "That revelation is called prophesy. And if you read the Old Testament, especially the book of Isaiah, you will find other detailed and specific prophesy about Jesus, his life and death. Those prophesies are part of the strong foundation of Christian faith. They make the Christmas story believable."

On our first day off from school, Dad, Liz, and I drove to a tree farm to cut a Christmas tree, as we always did. We found a big one and the workers helped tie it to the roof of our car. We all helped set it up and trim it in the evening. Then Dad and I put the Lionel train set together. The train ran around the base of the tree and under a cardboard tunnel that Dad had bought with the train set many years ago.

Mom's parents were coming to celebrate Christmas with us this year. Mom was unusually busy in the kitchen. I guess she wanted to prove that she had learned a lot from Grandma. I liked Grandpa and Grandma McDonald. They had six children, so we had a lot of uncles and aunts on that side of the family.

Grandma liked to tell stories about Mom when she was a little girl. Her hair was grey now, but Mom said it had been as red as hers is when Grandma was younger. Grandpa didn't have much hair, except around the edges, but he had a great sense of humor. He loved to tell jokes, and he always had a couple of brand-new ones when we saw him. They didn't visit very often, because they lived in Rochester, New York.

Christmas was special that year because our grandparents stayed almost a week. They came to church to see our program. We sat up late talking about family events. On Christmas morning we gathered in the living room to open presents. I got a pair of skis, and Dad promised he would teach me how to ski. He had used in the army, because his unit was in the Alps. He even kept his short army skis when he came home. Liz got a new clarinet; she was going to join the junior the high band. Lady got a new Steelers sweater to wear in cold weather. Grandpa brought her a box of treats.

Our grandparents had to leave a few days after Christmas. Before they left, I showed Grandpa my essay on the French and Indian War. He read it and told me it was excellent, and he said I could become a writer someday. It was a little sad waving goodbye as they got in the car to go back home. But we still had more than a week off school, and we resumed family sharing time. One evening Liz said she had something to share. I could tell Dad was very glad she spoke up. He told her to take all the time she wanted.

Liz said, "It won't take that long. It's just that I was sad to see Grandma and Grandpa leave, and I am sad that we finished the family history from the trunk. It was so much fun to read the old letters and visit historic places. I wonder what we can do now that would be as good as that."

We sat in silence for a minute. Then Mom said, "There are some things that Dad and I would like to tell you about that happened when we were young, like our home life, how we met, and things like that. If Dad wants to, he could tell you some World War II stories." She looked at Dad.

Dad paused a moment, like he was thinking hard. "Some of those memories are still difficult for me to talk about. But I think there are other things you might be interested in."

Liz said, "Sure, anything you want to talk about would be great."

So, for the next few days at sharing time Mom or Dad would tell us something about their lives before we were born. We learned more about our grandparents, Mom's big family and Dad's little one, and what life was like in the "30s during the Great Depression. What I really wanted to hear about was World War II.

Mom was the first one ready to talk about her family. "As you might or might not know, I was born in 1921 in Rochester, New York. Grandpa was running a construction company. They built houses, and small business offices. We were doing well, and I was treated like a princess. My sister and two brothers were as spoiled as I was. But the stock market collapsed in 1929, and Dad's investments disappeared almost overnight. He had some loans from the bank that had to be paid monthly; but people stopped buying houses, so we had very little income."

"We could have lost our house, but the bank agreed to accept some development land Dad owned in exchange for our mortgage; so at least we had a place to live. Many people did lose their homes. We had a tight budget. All of us kids helped Mom plant vegetables in our large yard. Dad did some handyman repair work for a few dollars here and there. Things got a little better in 1937, so Dad started back in the construction business. I graduated in 1938 and worked for a year as a grocery store clerk and saved all my money for college."

Liz said, "That's where you met Dad, right?"

Mom said, "Yes. Choosing to go to Bucknell was my best decision, because I met your Dad when I was a sophomore. He was a junior. He played on the baseball team, and one of my girlfriends took me to a game. She had her eye on the catcher. We walked over near the dugout after the game and talked with three players—her catcher, and two of his friends. I focused on the guy with the big grin. He was funny from the first day we met. I asked what position he played and he said he would really like to get to first base with me because he had already struck out with two sophomore girls. I couldn't resist his kind eyes and his humor.

"We were 'going steady' within a month. That meant we were not dating other people. He let me wear his letterman's sweater. I found out that he parents took him to church regularly. He was a Christian, and that meant a lot to me. We wrote to each other during the summer and resumed our dating in the fall. But World War II interrupted all of our plans in December. Dad finished off his semester and signed up for the army in January. It was a difficult parting, but I told him he was doing the right thing and that we could still write letters to each other."

I interrupted to ask whether the army had a post office. Dad explained how mail was handled by the military. The post office and the Department of Defense work together. And he said Mail Call was always a welcome break when the soldiers received their letters.

Liz asked Mom whether she continued to go to college when Dad went into the army. She said she finished the year. The next summer she went to work in the Rochester Kodak plant typing up war bonds. It was long hours and pretty boring, but it paid well and was an important way to help finance the high cost of the war. The government printed up bonds and people paid money knowing that the government would buy back the bonds and pay interest on them when the war ended.

Mom said, "Dad and I wrote back and forth for several months. Then his letters slowed down. I thought it was because of his deployment overseas. I prayed that he would come back safely.

It was a long two years. Dad wrote about once a month, sometimes less. But, you know that we eventually got married, so there's nothing to worry about, right? We need to get our chores done, so we'll talk about how that happened tomorrow."

The next evening Mom picked up right where she had left off, "When Dad came back to school in 1944, he was not the same. He had lost that quick wit and big smile. I worried about him and wanted to talk with him about why he seemed so serious. But he didn't want to talk about the military. So, we just kept distracted by other things."

Dad broke in, "You mother was so patient with me. I don't know what I would have become without her. I knew it was the horrible scene of war that I couldn't get off my mind and trying to forget was not working. They say time heals wounds, and it did make a difference, along with a lot of prayer. By the spring of my senior year, I was feeling more like my old self, and I proposed to your mom. She knew how to stir up my funny side, so she said she would marry me if I promised to laugh out loud at least once a day."

Mom told us that they were married in Rochester in March. There wasn't much planning, and the wedding was a pretty simple one at her church. They didn't have money for a honeymoon, but Dad's parents gave them $25 and other wedding gifts added $60. So, they took a little trip to New England and Dad got to see Plymouth Rock, where the Pilgrims landed. She liked walking on the beach and watching the wild life. Dad' car that wasn't too reliable, so the best thing about the trip was that it didn't break down.

They had enough money to rent a small apartment in Lewisburg near the university. After the school term ended, Dad started looking for a teaching job in the area. Shortly before September a small county district hired him to teach junior high history and civics. He started the first week of September. Mom worked at a local florist shop. She promised to talk about when we were born tomorrow.

The next evening Mom remembered what she had promised to tell us. She said that by July she knew was carrying a baby. If it was a girl they would call her Elizabeth. The doctor said the baby would be born before Christmas. Sure enough, Elizabeth arrived on December 12th, just a few days earlier than expected. Mom said Liz did everything a little before she was expected to, like walking at 9 months, reading before starting school, and already wanting to drive a car.

Dad was hoping the next baby would be a boy, and he got his wish nearly two years later. Jacob was a name both Dad and Mom liked; it was just a coincidence that Jacob was a frequently chosen name in the Klund ancestry. Mom said that as a little kid I was always curious and had a big imagination. I laughed and told them that I was hoping to find pirate treasure in the old trunk and was very disappointed when it turned out to be just paper.

Dad said, "Yes, but those papers mean a lot more to us than mere money."

A few days after we started back to school, Dad told us he was ready to talk about the war. He even brought some papers and notes. "First," he said, "you need to know some background about the war. I'll keep it short. The two world wars are connected. The peace treaty at the end of World War I created real trouble for Europe. It assessed millions of dollars of penalties on Germany that Germany could not afford to pay. President Wilson was more interested in a League of Nations to keep the peace than in the practical results. So, the U.S. ended up making loans to help Germany pay its war debt, but that just postponed the problem.

For a while everything seemed to be OK. Americans went on a spending spree in the 1920s. Radios, cars, and new electric appliances could all be bought on credit. Many people bought stock in American companies, raising the prices far above what the companies were worth. That all ended suddenly when the market collapsed in 1929. Our economy slowed, sales declined, people lost jobs."

"A Great Depression started here and became a world-wide calamity. Out of that crisis came new leaders. Franklin Roosevelt was elected president. He tried all kinds of government programs to end the depression. Nothing seemed to work."

"Adolf Hitler rose to power in Germany. Breaking the terms of the treaty they had signed after World War I, Germany began to rebuild its army. Hitler's National Socialists seized power and directed their economy. Freedom was lost. The NAZIs controlled everything. Then they blamed all of Germany's troubles on the Jews."

Liz asked, "Why did he blame it on the Jews?"

Dad said, "Good question. There is no easy answer. Hitler took advantage of German resentment for the penalties of the treaty that ended World War I. He chose to believe that Germans had been betrayed by German Jews. And he promoted the idea that Germans are a master race and the Jews were inferior."

"The German people were desperate for a leader that would end their depression. Hitler was bold and decisive. He was also deceptive. When his party seized power, he broke the terms of the treaty and began to rearm Germany. Then he began to expand Germany. He seized Austria in 1938, and then he invaded part of Czechoslovakia. When he invaded Poland, that started World War II. Italy, Germany, and Japan were the Axis powers. England, France, and the Soviet Union were the Allies. The U.S. was determined not to go to war again."

I said, "So why did we go to war?"

Dad answered, "Roosevelt began to restrict our sales of iron and other things to Japan because they were allies of Germany. Japan bombed our naval base, Pearl Harbor, Hawaii on December 7, 1941. President Roosevelt called it a "day that will live in infamy." We declared war on Japan."

Dad explained, "When we went to war, I was finishing the first semester of my sophomore year at Bucknell. Harriet and I had met and had a few dates. I thought I might be drafted into the army, and I believed it was better to volunteer. So, I said goodbye to your mom and made a short visit with your grandma and grandpa to tell them I was leaving. It was really hard to leave, because Grandpa was not in good health. But he said he was proud of me and gave me a long hug."

"I took a train from Pittsburgh to Charlotte, North Carolina and a bus to Camp Butner. After several months of training we were transported across the Atlantic to the Mediterranean and Morocco, North Africa. I was in General Mark Clarks, 5th Army. We spent many months preparing to invade Sicily and then cross to Italy."

"In early September we crossed the Mediterranean and stormed the beaches of Salerno at 3:30 in the morning. The plan was to surprise the Germans, but they were ready for us. They had land mines, barbed wire, and machine-guns aimed at the beaches. But we had help from the British and American ships offshore firing. When our air force and another English army came to support us, the Germans began to retreat."

"We fought our way to Naples by October. Rome was about a hundred miles away. That's when I heard about Ernie Pyle. He was a war correspondent, writing about what he saw for the people back home. Almost every American knew about him. I borrowed his book *Brave Men* from the school library. Mom can read this page for us. It's about the men I knew in Italy." She took the book and Dad showed her the place to start.

> *The fighting on the mountaintop almost reached the caveman stage sometimes. Americans and Germans were frequently so close that they actually threw stones at each other. Many more hand grenades were used than in any other phase of the Mediterranean war. And you have to be pretty close to throw hand grenades.*
>
> *Rocks played a big part in the mountain war. Men hid behind rocks, threw rocks, slept in rock crevices, and even were killed by flying rocks.*
>
> *When an artillery shell bursts on a loose rock surface, rock fragments are thrown for many yards.*

Dad told Mom to skip a few lines and pointed where to begin again.

> *When soldiers came down the mountain out of battle they were dirty, grimy, unshaven and weary. They looked ten*

years older than they were. They didn't smile much. But the human mind and body recover rapidly. After a couple of days down below they began to pick up. It was a sight to see a bunch of combat soldiers after they had shaved and washed up. As one said, "We all look sick after we've cleaned up, we're so white."

Dad told Mom that was a good place to stop, and he asked us how we liked Ernie Pyle's writing. Everyone agreed that it made the war seem closer to us. So, Dad said he would keep the book at home for a while, in case we wanted to read a little more.

Dad ended his war story by telling us he lost two good friends in the Italian campaign and that Mom was right, he was not his usual self when he returned to Bucknell.

The next day it snowed long and hard. After it let up a little, Dad took me to a nearby hill and began to teach me how to ski. After a few falls, I became more stable and enjoyed gliding silently down the small slopes. There is such a great feeling of freedom and power, gliding down a hill and controlling your path, while the wind blows against your face. We had no ski lift, so we got plenty of exercise climbing back up the hill. Dad told me that after I felt comfortable on steeper slopes, we would go to a mountain where they did have a ski lift. I practiced turning and stopping diligently, so that time would come soon.

In mid-February we had a heavy rain. When Mom went upstairs she heard dripping in the spare bedroom. She went in and saw wet puddles on the night stand and carpet. It was coming from the ceiling. Mom put a bucket and a pan under it told Dad about it that evening. He was concerned about the roof leaking, and he knew that the old shingles should be replaced. The problem was the we didn't have the money to pay for it. So, we began to pray about this in our family sharing time.

One evening after dinner, Mom said she had a thought about how to pay for the roof. We were all ears. Mom told Dad that something in the trunk could have antique value. Maybe we should check out the old 1812 Baltimore newspaper with the original "Star Spangled Banner." It could be collectable. Dad said that was a great idea, and he would ask some teachers at the school where he should go in Pittsburgh to inquire about it.

Dad had three antique dealers' addresses when he drove to Pittsburgh on Saturday. When he came home, he told us that he found a dealer who was going to do some research on the newspaper and would call us as soon as he knew its value. We were hopeful this would turn out to be an answer to our prayers.

The call came on Wednesday evening. The dealer said that he estimated the newspaper to be worth between $3,000 and $5,000! And he was willing to pay $3500 for it. When Dad told us we all celebrated like crazy. Dad laughed and told me that my treasure chest was worth more than anyone could have guessed. He estimated that a new roof would only cost $500. That would leave more than enough to have the house painted, which it really needed. We would still have some money to save for college for Liz and me! Mom suggested that since this was an answer to prayer we should make a big donation to our church building fund. They agreed on $300.

At our next family sharing time Dad told us that selling the Baltimore newspaper was the right decision. "But," he said, "the rest of the contents of the trunk should stay in the family. It was a precious gift that so many people had preserved for us. We should honor their intentions and preserve it for future generations. That means you, Liz and Jacob."

We agreed. Liz smiled and said, "It should be preserved by the first one of us to get married."

I said, "It should be preserved by the person who found the trunk."

Dad laughed, out loud as usual and said, "That is a decision that you two can make thirty years from now. Until then Mom and I will do the preserving."

CHAPTER 11

Reflections

I AM SKIPPING AHEAD several years, although it will leave many things unsaid about those "happy days" when Liz and I were growing up in Pleasant Hill. I do have vivid memories of much more than I have told you. But now let me take you with me into the 1960s.

Liz graduated from high school in 1963 and planned to enroll at Westminster College. During the summer, Grandpa MacDonald called and told us that Grandma was in the hospital. Mom told him that we would be there in Rochester the next day. So, we packed our suitcases and left early in the morning.

When we arrived at Grandpa's house, we knew he was very anxious about Grandma. We all went together to Rochester General Hospital. On the way, Grandpa told us that Grandma had been having many headaches for several months. The doctors told him that she had a kind of brain cancer. When we arrived, Grandpa and Mom went into her room to visit. When they came back out to the visiting room, I could tell that Mom was worried.

She talked quietly with Dad for a little while. Finally, she said that Dad, Liz, and I could go into Grandma's room for a few minutes, but she was on a lot of medication and might be sleeping. She was barely awake. I asked Dad if I could give her a hug. He said ok, but I should be gentle. Liz and I each went over to the bedside and gave Grandma a kiss. She smiled at us but didn't say anything. When we went back out of the room, Grandpa and mom went back in and stayed for a long time.

The next morning, Grandpa called the hospital to see whether we could visit again. They told him that Grandma had died during the night. We all gathered in the living room and cried together. Grandpa hugged me and Liz and told us that it was ok. He knew she had been in a lot of pain and now she was finally free and in heaven. Mom came over to the couch and sat next to him. It was so quiet that I could hear a clock ticking, but seemed that time had stopped.

By the late afternoon, Dad and Mom were helping Grandpa make funeral arrangements. Liz and I sat on the living room couch looking through the family photo albums. Grandma was certainly a beautiful woman when she got married. Liz left the room for a few minutes. When she came back, I asked her where she went. She said that she went to talk with Dad and Mom about staying here with Grandpa for a few weeks after the funeral. Mom had to go back to work and Dad needed to take care of the house.

So, the three of us went back home and let Liz stay with Grandpa. Mom said she was so proud of her for volunteering to do that. We agreed. Dad said that Liz had so much compassion for suffering people and that's probably one of the reasons she wanted to become a doctor.

So, Liz entered Westminster College as a pre-med student in the Fall of 1963. I didn't realize how much I would miss her. It took months for me to adjust to being the only kid at home. When she came back for Christmas and summer vacations, she had so much to tell us. Those were such happy times together.

I graduated from high school in 1965 and spent a year with the Pennsylvania National Guard before I entered Capital University in Columbus, Ohio. I wanted to study history and law. I had gotten interested when Dad talked about court cases that dealt with freedom of religion. I even wrote a paper on that in high school government class. When I graduated from Capital, I was hired by a firm that handles cases for churches, Christian schools, and other religious associations.

Liz and I both made frequent visits home to see Mom and Dad. They were still living in Grandma's old Victorian house. Lady was there too, and they were so glad to have her companionship. Grandpa MacDonald often came and stayed for weeks, especially around the holidays. One of our favorite things to do in those evenings with Grandpa was taking Lady on a long walk.

As Dad had predicted, two Supreme Court cases in the 1960s removed prayer and Bible reading from the public schools. The first was *Engle* v. *Vitale* in 1962. The Court ruled that the State of New York had violated the First Amendment's separation of church and state when it composed an official school prayer and encouraged its recitation in public schools. Another case was *Abington School District* v. *Schempp* in 1963. That case challenged school sponsored Bible reading. It was accompanied by *Murray* v. *Curlett* in which Madlyn Murray had brought suit against the Baltimore Public Schools where her son was enrolled. The Court ruled that school sponsored Bible reading was also unconstitutional for the same First Amendment reason. Murray went on to be America's most recognized atheist, enjoying so much media exposure despite her seriously flawed and bizarre lifestyle.

Looking back on those cases, the Supreme Court decisions seemed very wrong to me at the time. I understood Dad's explanation that the First Amendment was not written to control a state's actions. It applied to the federal government. Of course, the Court did not see it that way. By the 1960s activist progressive judges were interpreting the Constitution very loosely.

Today, it seems practical to believe that forcing students into a religious exercise was not going to change them much. Sadly, the removal of a Christian influence in public schools has affected young people. As respect for teachers declined and violence increased, some Christian parents began to move their students into church-sponsored schools, or they tried home-schooling.

Let me say something else about the 1960s. Some people believe that a time of innocence and hope turned to a time of anger and violence in the 60s because of the assassinations of President Kennedy and Dr. Martin Luther King. These assassinations did shock the nation. They were, indeed, a sign of troubled times.

The popular explanation for the rebellious 60s is that young people rejected their parents' values because they didn't offer an adequate foundation for the changing times. The truth is that young people were *led* to reject their parents' values. The civil rights movement drew attention to generations of discrimination, and the Vietnam War divided the nation. Seeds of youth discontent over these issues were watered by rock and roll musicians like Bob Dylan, liberal college professors, and the national media. These new idols of young people promoted secular humanism, a worldview based on atheism, naturalism, evolution, and ethical relativism. Here is a brief look at each of these ideologies.

Atheism simply rejects the belief in any god. Naturalism says that nature is the governing force of the universe. Evolution claims that all life began with a single cell and developed into more and more complex organisms over a long period of time by natural selection. Ethical relativism says that we develop our beliefs of right and wrong, good and bad, based on our needs and those of the society around us. There are no absolute values.

All of these assumptions suggest that religious faith is defenseless as a foundation for society. That is not what our founders believed. But today, is religious faith defenseless? I remember Dad explaining to us the real defense of our Christian belief system. He said it all hinges on the person of Jesus. His existence is challenged by very few people. His claim to be the "Son of God," is the issue. The church survived over the centuries because it believed He was who He said He was; that He was crucified, died, and rose again. No one else has made such a claim, If that is so, everything He says is true, because life and death are the biggest mystery.

Jesus supported the Old Testament account of the creation and origin of man. The early Christians staked everything on the belief that He was divine and that His crucifixion is the key event of all human history. Those early followers suffered rather than to deny what they knew to be true, that He rose from the dead. Peter and Paul were among thousands who met death in Rome defending that belief.

The nation's founding documents rest on Christian principles. The Declaration of Independence says, "We hold these truths to be self-evident, that all men are created equal, that they are endowed by their Creator with certain unalienable Rights, that among these are Life, Liberty and the pursuit of Happiness." Without that foundation, there is no real support for rights, liberty, or equality.

How did these principles develop in the Western World? They emerged from the Protestant Reformation. We can trace the principle that the law reigns supreme to Samuel Rutherford, author of *Lex Rex* or the *Law and the Prince* published in 1644. Rutherford, a Scot, believed that scripture, not the king, was the standard. Parliament charged him with high treason. He died before he could be sentenced.

John Witherspoon, a disciple of Rutherford, and a Presbyterian minister educated at Edinburg University, came to America. He taught the principles of *Lex Rex* to James Madison at the College of New Jersey (now Princeton University). He was the only member of the clergy to sign the Declaration of Independence, and he played a key role in the Continental Congress, both directly and indirectly. He taught ten American cabinet officers, twenty-one senators, thirty-nine members of Congress, and twelve governors.

James Madison has been called the *"Father of the Constitution."* His college teacher, John Witherspoon's, influence played a major role in the drafting of the Constitution. This is the heritage that came under attack beginning with Charles Darwin's theory of evolution.

When the foundations of our nation were shaken in the 1960s, I had many conversations with Dad. He was a good advisor to me, but he still felt that he should have gotten more involved in Christian education himself. Still, he has been a great support for my decisions. I should also mention how much I appreciate Mom. In many ways, she was the foundation of our home. It is my prayer that many more children will be afforded the strength of a Christian family that Liz and I had.

The Project

A brief parable

ONE DAY A FAMILY, saw a large box on their front porch. It had their address, but no return address. They were afraid to open it, but being inquisitive, the father got a sharp knife and slit it open. There was a little packing material on top and the young son carefully pulled it away. Underneath was a pile of loose parts. They looked for instructions but could find none.

They talked about what to do. The father decided they should try to put it together; it would be a fun project, and they could discover what it was as they worked on it. So, they put it in the center of the room and worked on it whenever they had time, individually or together. Once a week, they got together and discussed the project.

At first nothing seemed to fit right; but one day the father saw a similarity in two pieces and managed to fit them together. Everyone celebrated that evening and they were energized to work harder. Every few days after that, someone found another piece that seemed to fit. Once in a while they would have to remove a piece because even it didn't quite fit, or it led nowhere.

By trial and error, they made progress. Every little success created enthusiasm. No one thought about where the box came from or why anymore. The project had taken on a life of its own. As the *construction evolved, the family became obsessed with the project. Then they found another box on the porch. More pieces had arrived. The family was unaffected. It no longer mattered how long it would take or even what the end result of the project could be. The only thing that they cared about was its evolution.*

They invited the neighbors to see what they were doing. Some neighbors joined in the effort. But a few asked questions like, "Who sent the box? Why was it sent to you? What do you think it's purpose is?" The family chose to allow anyone to help as long as they did not ask such questions. One neighbor even said that he had a book that explained the origin of boxes like this. They laughed at that impossibility. The father told the neighbor he was not welcome to contribute or even observe the process because he didn't appreciate the meaning of its evolution. The family, and Mr. Darwin, the father, agreed. The source of the box or its purpose did not matter. The Project was their life.

Isaac Newton saw no conflict between science and Christianity. In fact, without faith, secular science deprives life of meaning and purpose. Albert Einstein once said: "There are only two ways to live your life. One is as though nothing is a miracle. The other is that everything is a miracle." The church, the home, and the Christian school are foundational to a warm, caring society. They remain the best alternative to THE PROJECT.